ALYS

THE TERRA MIRUM CHRONICLES

ALYS

THE TERRA MIRUM CHRONICLES

Kiri Callaghan

Doce Blant Publishing

WWW.DOCEBLANT.COM

Published by
Doce Blant Publishing, Dana Point, CA 92629
www.doceblant.com

Cover by Fiona Jayde Media

ISBN-10: 0-9978913-9-4
ISBN-13: 978-0-9978913-9-3
Library of Congress Control Number: 2016956363

Printed in the United States of America
www.doceblant.com

Books by Kiri Callaghan

The Terra Mirum Chronicles

Red

Puck

Alys

Changeling

A special thanks to Lewis Carroll, for Alice's Adventures in Wonderland. These stories helped me become who I am today, and without them, of course, this story would not be possible.

My eternal gratitude to William Shakespeare, whose works taught me the true magic in words.

To Joel, who may have lost his battle with his Nightmare, but inspired me to never stop fighting my own.

We love and miss you. Always.

PROLOGUE

They locked the doors.
The darkness remained outside his window,
but it seeped in through hers.
He inhaled, She choked.
She tensed, He relaxed.
They sank into a seat on the bed, She facing
the East, He the West.
It couldn't end now.
Thank God, it was.
She raised a hand to her mouth—He raised
a gun to his.
Trembling and steady.
Hands clenched on the sheets, tendons
straining beneath the skin.
Pain and preparation.
Two deep breaths, a single exhalation.
Thunder and silence.
They fell back to the bed, prone and lifeless.
Two hearts stopped at the exact same
moment.
They had nothing in common in life, but
what they shared in death would forge a
bond between the worlds of mind and matter.

Chapter 1

THE NIGHTMARE QUEEN

They did not bother to wake Oswin before they yanked him from his bed. The rough grip around his arms startled him out of slumber, but his coherent thoughts were not fast following. He blinked insistently to clear the blur from his vision, and his feet fumbled to match the pace of the steps to either side of him. He felt clumsy and out of sync against the militant rhythm of each footfall.

Soldiers.

He rolled his head to look to one side of him, but the identity of his captors only drew more questions.

Not soldiers. Guards. His guards.

"What's going on?" It was a noble effort at sounding in control, but even a prince will have a hard time appearing composed when still half asleep and wearing his nightclothes.

Neither guard answered, nor acknowledged him. The way they continued on had a stiff, clockwork-toy quality.

"I demand an explanation." Oswin tried to yank himself away, but their grip was like iron shackles. "Answer me! I order you, as the crowned prince of Terra Mirum. You have no right to — "

It was then he noticed the others. The rest of the castle had also been taken from their beds and were being guided — or dragged, depending on their level of cooperation—in the same direction by other palace guards. Oswin planted his feet, locked his stance, and held his ground for a few precious seconds before he was jerked forward again by the guards. Their forcefulness knocked him off his feet and they slid behind him.

Boots on either side of him marched in perfect time down the stairs and into the Great Hall.

All the people wrested from their beds were gathered there. *Everyone* was filed in alongside everyone else: maids, lords, even other guards. There was no discrimination of status, profession or gender.

He couldn't decipher the reason behind any of it. No one appeared injured. In fact, he saw no signs of violence at all. While a relief, it was perhaps the most confusing aspect of the lot. Oswin knew war and revolution, and they were never bloodless. Nobles were kept alive only to be later used as bargaining chips, and anyone considered politically useless was killed or neutralized by other means. Prisoners weren't hauled from their beds to simply be put in a lineup...so why had the servants been spared?

Moonlight glowed through the great windows, a pale light that shone on hundreds of frightened faces lined up like prisoners awaiting execution.

The last marching foot stopped and all sound died as if a scream of silence were echoing through the room.

The air grew stiff and settled into a kind of rigor mortis, cold and lifeless. It was a deathly kind of stillness, so sudden and haunting it startled the breath back into people.

Oswin struggled to inhale.

The guards' grip on his arms became so tight he could feel their pulses pumping against his skin, and for a moment, his mind considered a strange phenomenon. Were their pulses in unison?

The silence shattered, and a strange sound echoed down the hallway.

Doom-tek.

And then another.

Doom-tek.

And another, and another, and another, until it became a continuous, steady rhythm. A strange, mechanical heartbeat. A heartbeat that filled the room and kept the time.

The guards at Oswin's side shoved him down. His knees made hard contact with the cold floor. He attempted to raise his head to look toward the heartbeat, but it was forced down again by a guard's hand. He stared at his own reflection in the marble. His eyes met their likeness in the floor, and he saw something in them he hadn't even realized was there: fear.

The heartbeat was getting louder—no, not louder—*closer*. It was some kind of footstep. And it was coming right towards him.

Doom-tek. Doom-tek. Doom-tek. Doom-tek.

He watched the toes of two high-heeled boots square with him, a train of ebony fabric pooling around them. His eyes moved up, taking in the rigid figure that stood before him.

She was more sculpture than creature. Her components suggested human features, yet they were far too hard and chiseled for him to believe she was actually made of flesh. Her skin was a stark, pale contrast against the black garment that clung to her. However, nothing unnerved him as much as the eyes locked onto his. Two black pools—endless—as dark and unending as The Nothing itself. There was no question in Oswin's mind: What stood before him now was no less than Nightmare.

"Hello, rabbit," she cooed.

"Who are you?" He spat out the demand before his mind had much time to think about it. His eyes widened as he looked further into hers, straining to find even a hint of light in them. "What are you doing here?"

Black-painted lips parted into the smallest of smiles, but his question went unanswered.

"You won't get away with this." He

grasped onto any defense his mind could muster. "Queen Aislynn will stop you. She's taken down far stronger armies—you will…" Oswin's eyes focused on something even more terrible than those of the Nightmare: an object far too familiar that rested atop her head as if it belonged there. The white gold crown glistened even in the dim light, twisting and curling around pearl and diamond insets. He knew that crown's intricate construction since his infancy. Oswin spoke again, softer. "Where is my mother?"

Her head tilted to the side ever so slightly with a satisfied exhalation. Her breath chilled the room like winter frost. "What is his name, my dear?"

A shadow of a creature limped to her side. It was hard to make out at first, bent over and quivering as it was, but Oswin realized that it was also something he recognized. "Father?"

King Erebus had once been a tower of strength, both great in physical stature and presence. He had led soldiers into battle, stood at Aislynn's side during The Great War itself, and had been heralded as one of Elan Vital's greatest warriors. That man was now unrecognizable. He cowered at the Nightmare's feet like a beaten dog. He looked weak and hollowed out, as if drained of life, his body aged well beyond the years it was designed to live. With a great but careful effort, as if the mere weight of his own head could snap his neck, he turned his gaze on his son, then craned it upwards toward the Nightmare. "Oswin."

His name was like a forgotten melody to the Nightmare, and the subtlest undulation rolled down her body, starting from her ear and slithering down to her toes. "Oswin."

Oswin's heartbeat faltered in its rhythm, and his breath caught. He struggled, and a wave of panic washed through him, but the grip on his arms only tightened. He felt the guards' nails digging into his skin through the thin fabric of his shirt.

"Oswin," the Nightmare said once more, firmer this time.

Again, his heartbeat stumbled, almost stopping long enough to match a new rhythm.

Magic. It was taking control. *She* was taking control.

He gritted his teeth, and his heart pounded at a pace he could not slow — like a drug running through his veins to coax him to sleep. He could hear the beat in his ears, and his body grew rigid with each thump.

At what he knew to be the Nightmare's behest, his eyes snapped open, forcing him to stare into the unblinking abyss of her own. "Now that you're listening." Her smile broadened.

Oswin felt sick but unable to move.

The Nightmare's hand reached out, and her fingertips stroked the top of Erebus's head like a pet. "Elan Vital is now in my control. Tomorrow I will bring your kingdom's fall. Starting with your public execution."

Oswin's own terror could not shake his heart out of the rhythm dictated by the Nightmare.

"Leave the rest but lock him up. Heart and all."

Chapter 2

Tea and Sympathy

Alyson Carroll awoke that morning feeling energized. For the first time in years she had slept completely through the night. Not only had her mind been undisturbed by the commonplace terrors that tormented her on other nights, but it had been a dreamless sleep. She left for work that morning cheerful, a skip in her step and a hum on her lips.

Blissful ignorance.

It was a drastic mood shift noticeable to the other waitresses as she dropped off her things in the backroom, and their reactions ranged from confused to even uncomfortable.

"Maybe she had her coffee before work?" One waitress shrugged to the other two.

"Maybe her mother finally kicked the bucket," the second muttered.

"Good morning, Alyson!" The third waitress pitched her voice higher in volume to alert her coworkers that Alys was re-entering the room.

"*Great* morning, MaryAnn." Alys tied her apron around her waist.

Susie's was not a fancy diner, but it was clean and well-lit, which was more than most establishments in Appleweed could boast. The light from the windows cast a warm, inviting glow that seeped through the fog that rolled in every morning from the harbor. It was the sort of place that guaranteed two things: hot food and strong coffee.

Susanne Bosk, the diner's proprietor and namesake, was neither warm nor inviting. She was a woman of business. A stout character with tight curls and deep-set brown eyes, she was a woman whom only a select few ever dared to call "Susie." She ran a tight ship—never opened late and never closed early. Her thin lips were stretched across her face and secured a toothpick at the corner of her mouth. That morning, the slightest hint of a good mood lingered somewhere in her expression. Its exact source was unidentifiable. It could have been a twinkle in her eye, or maybe her lips held just a vague, upturned twitch, but it was there. Alys's mood was contagious today.

Alys swayed back and forth to the muffled tones of the jukebox in the far corner as she went about her morning prep. She set the tables one by one as the tantalizing scent of bacon and coffee filled the entire restaurant. For once, she gave a genuine smile as customers filed in and she took their orders. She couldn't help it; that morning was nothing but promises of a fantastic day.

That morning *lied*.

If Alys hadn't been too preoccupied with refills to notice the sheriff enter, she might have realized that he was an hour early for his usual seven o'clock breakfast. However, Sheriff Moss had the kind of voice that caught your ear, which no doubt was helpful on the job, but also tended to invoke unintentional eavesdropping.

"Mornin', Susie." Moss slid into one of the chairs at the bar with an ease only achieved with years of repetition. There was an unusual weariness to his demeanor.

"Sheriff." Susanne leaned on the counter. "Awful early to be seeing you. Still want your usual?"

"Coffee." He stared hard at the counter. "Just coffee. Black. Don't got the stomach for anything else this morning. Haven't slept yet, had to pull a double."

A mug clinked onto the counter, and Susanne filled it with coffee in a manner that seemed more akin to a bartender pouring a stiff drink. "Something happened." It wasn't a question, but she still expected answers.

Alys had a keen sense of hearing. Knowing what was worth listening to had been a key survival tool growing up. In a town where nothing ever happened, an event that not only kept the sheriff up all night but left him visibly shaken was definitely something to give one pause.

Moss lowered his voice and leaned in, but nothing in the world could have stopped Alys from hearing his words as she rounded back behind the counter for another pot of coffee. "You know the Lewis' boy?"

Alys's heart stopped.

"That queer kid?" Susanne asked and quirked an eyebrow. "Sure, he's in a couple of times a week. Doesn't order much, but he's all right enough. What's he done?"

"Swallowed one of his daddy's guns sometime around five last night. Blew a hole clear through the back of his head. Wasn't pretty."

Glass shattered.

Both Susanne and the sheriff were startled out of what they assumed had been a private conversation and saw the broken coffee pot before they noticed the waitress who had dropped it.

"Alyson!" Susanne turned the most exasperated glare in her direction. "What are you doing?"

Alys jumped, looked at Susanne and the sheriff, then down at the splatter of glass and coffee at her feet. "S-sorry."

Susanne tossed her a towel. "Go on. We aren't lacquering the floor with it." She turned back around to the sheriff.

The conversation continued, but Alys didn't hear it. Everything seemed far away and garbled, like she'd stuck her head underwater. Her fingers and knuckles whitened around the towel, and she sank into a crouch. The world swayed, and she gripped the cupboard handle for balance. She felt motion sick. She looked at the murky puddle and the reflection of her own honey-brown eyes stared back at her. What was she supposed to be doing?

Her vision blurred as she watched the coffee separate into squares against the white tile, forming a checkerboard pattern. The shards of glass grew and twisted upwards, forming pawns, knights and bishops. She took in the image of the chessboard that now lay before her, knowing she hadn't the slightest idea what to do with it.

"Alys."

She looked up at the boy sitting on the steps beside her.

Charlie Lewis had the sort of face girls in school would have swooned over if they weren't too busy repeating the same homophobic garbage their parents whispered to each other. His bone structure was strong, his build was athletic, and he had a tousled mess of loose blond curls that he was always brushing from his eyes. His mouth twitched in a smile. "Move."

Alys fidgeted, her fingers hovering over each individual piece.

"Try to think a few moves ahead."

"This game is stupid," Alys said.

"You just don't want to lose again."

"You're right. I don't!"

Charlie pursed his lips and cocked his head to the side, giving a meaningful look towards her, then the board.

Alys let out an exasperated sigh and moved a knight before recoiling from the board and covering her face as if she expected it to explode.

He chuffed a laugh and moved his queen forward, taking one of her pawns.

Alys stared, her eyes peeking through her fingers. She dropped her hands as something dawned on her. She felt her excitement mounting, a wide grin spreading over her face as she moved her own queen forward to topple his. "Checkmate!" The word was shouted at the top of her lungs, while throwing her hands up in triumph.

"What?" Charlie jerked forward from his relaxed slump, eyeing the board. He looked over every piece, and his face crumpled in disbelief. "Nu-uh. Where?"

"Ha-ha, ha-ha, ha-*ha*!" Alys waved the black queen's piece under his nose in a very *neener, neener, neener*-type fashion.

"Alys." Charlie pinched the bridge of his nose, but it wasn't clear if he was frustrated or just trying to suppress laughter. "That's not checkmate."

"Uh-huh." But her voice was already losing its confidence, and she pulled the piece to her like it was delicate and needed protection. "I have your most powerful piece... it's totally a checkmate."

"Most powerful, maybe, but not the most significant. You can still win without a queen. Like this." He moved a black pawn and removed the white king. "Checkmate."

Alys's mouth opened, closed, opened again, and then her face scrunched into a scowl.

"In the end, there are really only kings and pawns." He tapped her nose with the king piece still in his hand. "Some just move fancier than others."

She tightened her grip on the queen still in her hand. "I hate chess."

"Give it time."

"I hate you."

Charlie laughed. "Alyson, your hand."

Alys blinked. "What?" She looked down, but she was no longer holding a chess piece at all. Her hand was curled around a shard of glass now dripping blood.

"Here, let me see it." Mary Ann took her hand in her own, removing the glass piece with a rag held between her fingers.

"It's fine."

"You're in shock."

Alys looked around her, disoriented. The world, the diner…what should have been familiar sights seemed alien now.

"Mom," the mousy girl called to Susanne, indicating the office where anything that they couldn't afford to get food-stained was kept. "Can you get the binder with the emergency contact info? I think we'll want to call her mother." She bit her lower lip, pressing the rag into Alys's hand after disposing of the glass.

Alys felt a lump form in her throat. Her emergency contact? Years ago when she'd first applied to the job, she'd put down the only person she could think of who would care if something happened to her—Charlie. "You can't…" She didn't get further than that. She'd meant to say, *you can't call him. You can't call him because he's dead,* but the words stuck and her voice felt tight.

"What?" Mary Ann asked as she helped her stand and lean back against the counter for balance as Susanne returned from the office with the notebook containing the employee contact information.

Alys cleared her throat, trying to suppress the rising anxiety. "You can't call him…"

"Alyson," Mary Ann tried to reason. "You need someone to take you to the emergency room—this may need stitches. You can't drive there by your—"

"Mary," Susanne spoke up from the notebook in her hands.

Alys could tell by the look on Susanne's face that she had just discovered her emergency contact was that same "queer kid" who blew a hole through the back of his head the previous night.

For the first time since she'd known her, Susanne Bosk looked shaken, even pale. She glanced from the book to her daughter and then to Alys. "Mary Ann is going to drive you to the emergency room, honey."

Susanne didn't even keep honey in the diner, let alone call anyone by it. The look she gave her was sympathetic, and Alys resented every glance she caught of it.

"I'll help you get her things." Susanne ushered Mary Ann into the office.

Alys knew it was a thinly veiled excuse for Susanne to explain the situation to her daughter, but at least it meant she wouldn't have to. This theory was only confirmed when Mary Ann remerged with both of their belongings and a far more solemn attitude.

Unnerving quiet followed their procession out of the diner, a quiet that burst into a quake of whispers as the door closed behind them.

Alys's car was a run-down 1995 Volkswagen Jetta. Two years ago, Alys had managed to scrounge up enough tip money to purchase it. It was battered, a little decrepit, and may have been white once in its life, but was now a perpetual dirty grey. It was unattractive, loud as hell, and the radio station flipped every time you used the turn signal, but it moved, and that was really all that mattered.

The two climbed in and Mary Ann struggled to start the engine.

"Cock it back, then forward." Alys rubbed her face with her clean hand, shifting in her seat. She wasn't used to sitting on the passenger's side. It felt wrong. Everything felt wrong.

"Is there any glass still in your hand?"

"No, I just grabbed a big piece." Alys removed the bloody handkerchief that Mary Ann had given her to examine her wound. It was barely even bleeding anymore. Now that it wasn't covered in blood, it looked a great deal more harmless—no more than a paper cut. It was almost disappointing. "I really don't need to go to the emergency room."

"Okay." Mary Ann paused between shifting gears from reverse to drive. "I'll just... take you home, then. I think I remember the address. Venice Avenue, right?"

"Yeah."

An awkward silence filled the car.

Mary Ann glanced over at her. "I'm sorry about your friend."

Alys didn't answer.

"You didn't have to come to work today. Mother would have under— "

"I didn't know." There was something humiliating about that admission.

"Oh." It seemed as if another silence would fall upon them, but Mary Ann began again. "Is there someone else you can call?"

Alys looked sidelong at her. Call for what?

Mary Ann fixed her eyes on the road ahead of them and shrank in her seat. "It's just...I read in my psychology class that after traumatic events, it's best not to be alone, so— "

"No."

"No?"

"No, there's no one I can call."

Mary Ann swallowed nervously. "At least you have your mother— "

"Stop the car," Alys said.

"What?"

"The *car*. Stop the car." Alys smacked her palm down repeatedly on the armrest, hostility rising in her tone. "*Stop the car!*"

Mary Ann slammed on the breaks, bringing them to a screeching halt.

Alys barely let the car stop before she threw her door open and was sprinting across a lawn and down the street — Charlie's street. Somewhere in the back of her mind she heard Mary Ann calling her name, but she ignored her. Her heart pounded in her own ears. Her feet connected with the concrete, unable to slow or stop.

Charlie's house seemed abandoned, the last of the police cars having left a few hours prior to give the family privacy. It was a grand house, remodeled recently and kept up to military standard cleanliness.

Alys flew up the steps of the large wrap-around porch, her hand balled into a fist, and banged on the door. "Open, god, please open."

The door did open, but it wasn't Charlie, and by sheer grace of some higher power, it wasn't his father, either.

"Alyson?" Karen Lewis' eyes were wider than usual and her whole form shuddered with her breathing as if the only thing holding her up was the door she held onto.

Even under normal circumstances, Charlie's mother was a small, timid woman, so Alys had no difficulty pushing past her.

"Wait!"

Alys climbed the stairs in twos, racing to get to the room before anyone could stop her. Thinking maybe, *just maybe*, it was all a lie. If she could just prove it, everything would go back to normal. She flung open Charlie's bedroom door at the end of the hall and stumbled inside.

Charlie spun around in his chair, his classic but crooked smile spreading across his face, warm and inviting. "Hey, you."

The heavy scent of bleach overpowered her senses and she sneezed, her head snapping downwards. When she looked up, the room was different: bare. The bed clothes were gone, some of the wallpaper was gone, but, worst of all—Charlie was gone.

Alys's shoulders slumped and her heart sank. "No..."

"Charles hasn't told anyone yet." Karen hovered just before the doorway as if scared to step over the threshold. She spoke simply. Much like Sheriff Moss, it was clear she also hadn't slept, and in her state of shock, she clung to the few facts she knew. "He's making arrangements with a home… The police only left… It wasn't long ago."

"Small town. Word travels fast."

Even though she wasn't facing the woman, she could imagine her brow knitting. "You shouldn't have had to hear like that."

"Charlie shouldn't have had to die like that." Without him, Charlie's room looked dark, almost dingy, like all of the air had been sucked out of the place. "I don't understand." She turned back to face Karen.

Karen's gaze was far off, her finger tips resting on her lips. "They'd had a fight that morning…they were always fighting. He went out for a few hours like he always did. He seemed fine. It seemed… normal." Her eyes slowly moved throughout the room, resting on the bed and looking through Alys to the desk. "I left to get groceries so I could have dinner ready for Charles at six… I… I don't think he wanted me to hear it. He was always thinking of me."

"Did he say anything?"

Karen shook her head and allowed herself to lean on the door frame with an exhalation that betrayed her exhaustion. "He was such a quiet boy. Always reading in his room… I told him I was leaving, and he hugged me goodbye. Told me he loved me. Same as always. Same as always…" Her eyes focused on Alys finally, remembering something. "He left something for you." Karen reached into her cardigan pocket and produced a folded piece of paper. Only then did her body shake with a sob and she crumpled against the door frame. "My baby…" She cradled the note to her chest. "My beautiful baby boy…" Her voice cracked, but her eyes had cried far too many tears in the past 14 hours to manage any more. They were dry and red.

Alys stepped forward to steady the woman and carefully guide her to her knees.

"He can't be gone, Alys. He was a good boy." Karen's fist tightened around the folded paper and she rocked slowly back and forth. "He was so smart."

"Mrs. Lewis," Alys said gently, looking towards the note.

Karen looked down at her own hand and relaxed her hold. She ran her fingers over it again with the kind of reluctance that suggested it may have been the only note Charlie had left at all. She swallowed, pursed her lips, and offered it to Alys.

A million things could have been written in that note, and she knew none of them were going to make that moment any better. And, yet, what frightened her even more about that letter were the millions of things that Charlie possibly didn't write. She opened it — it wasn't a full sheet of paper, a scrap at best, only folded twice. He'd signed it with the same, almost flamboyant, flourish he always did, but the note itself was simple:

Tell Alys I'm sorry.

Chapter 3

RELEASING THE RABBIT

The cell was cold, dank, and heavy with the stench of mildew. Oswin couldn't fathom how so much moisture could seep in through the mortar. The walls, the ceiling, even the floor, seemed to be oozing water — if it *was* water.

The whole dungeon had been long out of use before that night. In an age of peace, it had become useless and had fallen into neglect.

Now, Oswin wished its upkeep had been better tended. He'd avoided sitting as long as possible, pacing back and forth, but, after a few hours, his legs began to ache and he took to leaning just one shoulder against the wall.

The only illumination came from the tiny window in the door, allowing him just enough light that he could make out the vague boundaries and filth of his cramped quarters. When he stood closer to the light, he could see the translucent puff of warm air that curled past his lips and nose with every exhalation. The air was both bitter cold and wet, and it left a film on his skin that he couldn't seem to wipe off.

His legs bent, giving way to the exhaustion he'd struggled with since they'd thrown him in here. He eased himself down onto the floor, eyes closing as his fingers met the ground. It had a slick, slimy, mucus-like texture. Oswin wasn't a squeamish man, but he was also not accustomed to spending large quantities of time in whatever it was that he was sitting in. He leaned his head against the wall behind him, feeling his muscles relax one by one as exhaustion won out over caring about whatever filth he might be lounging in.

He replayed the night's events over and over again in his mind, still having trouble believing them to be any more than phantoms of a wild and unnatural imagination.

Nightmare: the only word that described her, and one that was full of uncertainty and fear. If, in fact, she was a Nightmare, she had escaped from The Nothing. There had always been rumors and myths of Nightmares escaping into Terra Mirum, but the idea that it had actually happened was unthinkable.

Why?

How?

He'd had plenty of time in that cell to think it over, but the situation was beyond his experience. No book existed, or would ever exist, that could have prepared him for this—not in the palace, not even in the Great Library in Thought.

Still, even more unnerving than the creature who wore his mother's crown was seeing his father bowing and scraping like The Nightmare's pet. Magic. That much was clear— the palace was so heavy with sorcery, even Oswin could feel it without experiencing it.

Experiencing it.

His heart palpitated at the memory until a series of long controlled breaths coaxed it back to regular speed.

His mother had been murdered, his father was being held captive in his own mind, and himself? Oswin hung his head and covered his face with his hands. His execution in the center of the capitol was imminent. He didn't even know how little time was left now. He couldn't see outside. Without even a view of the moon's place in the sky — or even just the sky itself--he had no hope of guessing how much time had passed. He could already imagine her magic forcing his limbs to march up to the executioner's block, the same way it had forced him to march into this very cell.

It was all going to end in a matter of hours. There wasn't a doubt in his mind. The peace in the Kingdom, the flourishing treaty between Fae and Dream, his family line, and everything his mother had fought for, would be gone. The Nightmare had already proven her power, and with nothing to stop her, it wouldn't be long before all of Terra Mirum was overrun.

A shadow blocked the light from the door.

Oswin wasn't sure how he hadn't heard them coming, since a jailer's keys were less than quiet things. He held his breath, and, for a moment, time hung in suspension.

The door clicked open.

Oswin stood, pushing his back up against

the wall, his hands balled into fists, and his stomach churning. This was it.

The silhouette that filled the doorway was neither The Nightmare nor even a guard, and when it addressed him, he did not recognize the voice at all. "Prince Oswin, I assume?" The tone was smooth, calm, friendly.

Oswin squinted, but he could not make out the physical details of his guest. "Who are you?"

The stranger's mouth pulled back, and his broad, toothy grin caught the light, almost glowing in the darkness. "A friend."

"A friend of *whom*?"

"As fond as I am of formalities, it would be within your best interest to come with me now and save introductions for after our escape."

"Escape?"

"I assumed you'd be familiar with the concept."

Chapter 4

YOU ARE NOW
LEAVING APPLEWEED

Alys's finger traced over Charlie's signature.
She re-read the note over a dozen times in
a matter of minutes. Her eyes stung and her
throat constricted as she exhaled: the tell-
tale precursors to an emotional breakdown.
She dismissed the feeling with a deep, controlled breath as she folded the note back
up and stuck it into her jeans pocket. "I'm
sorry." It was such a useless offering, but it
was all she had. She looked back to Karen
cautiously, finally feeling shame for barging
in. "I shouldn't have come…not like this. I
just…I had to see for myself." She began to
stand, offering her hand to help Karen up.

Karen nodded numbly. "Am I a bad mother?"

The question forced Alys to pause. She looked down at the woman still crumpled on the floor, unsure of what to say.

"Was it my fault?"

They were weighted questions. Ones that demanded a delicacy and tact that Alys wasn't emotionally equipped to provide. She thought of Charlie and what he would have wanted her to say. "No." She examined the way the shadows cast a bluish hue across the right side of the older woman's pained and sallow face. There were some things even concealer couldn't completely hide. For the first time, signs of Charles Sr.'s abuse didn't scare her. She didn't flinch away. She felt angry. "But I think it's terribly appropriate the gun he used to end his life belonged to your husband."

Karen looked away and the shadows on her face darkened.

"He may not have pulled the trigger, Mrs. Lewis, but we both know he contributed to Charlie's death."

"Please stop," Karen whispered, her eyes fixed almost desperately on the wallpaper.

Alys swallowed hard and just stood there for what seemed like minutes.

Neither said anything.

Alys let her hand drop to her side uselessly. "I loved your son very, very much, Mrs. Lewis. He meant everything in the world to me. He was family." Her voice was careful, soft, and she was all too aware of the eggshells she had chosen to stomp through. "But I still can't even imagine what you're going through right now, and it's heartless of me to think I can." She turned towards the stairs, knowing there was little else to say but, "I'm so sorry for your loss. I...I won't be bothering you anymore."

"The funeral will be on Thursday," the woman piped up. Karen looked back at Alys and her mouth struggled into a sad but compassionate smile. "I'm sure he would have wanted you there."

Alys cleared her throat and unknowingly mimicked Karen's tight-lipped and mirthless smile. "Thank you, but I don't think I can. I'm sorry for the intrusion." She shoved her hands in her sweatshirt pockets and headed out the front door.

The misty air was starting to roll in from the harbor, a storm not far behind.

Alys found the cool breeze a welcome relief after her escape from a house so still.

"Alyson!" Mary Ann called from the street—she'd been circling the block since Alys ran off. She looked scared half to death. "A-are you okay?" The mousy girl's eyes focused on the name on the mailbox and widened. "Is this where he lived and...?"

Alys gestured for Mary Ann to get back into the car. "Let's go."

The car roared to life like an old lawn mower and sputtered down the lane towards the main street. It was an otherwise silent ride. Alys leaned her head against the cool glass of the window, letting her eyes lose focus on the world around her while Mary Ann white-knuckled the steering wheel. She felt raw.

The Carroll household resided in a neighborhood the politer townsfolk called "the less kempt part of Appleweed."

Alys called it "the swamp" on account that it was closer to sea level than the rest of town, and when it rained enough, the streets were completely submerged. The sidewalk was ruptured with cracks, the grass was always overgrown, and gravel was piled over the grey mud to imitate driveways.

The car chugged along the street until it came to number 1016. The second "1" slanted to the left regardless of how many times Alys had tried to correct it.

Crooked concrete steps wound up a small, uneven incline that gave the illusion that the house on top was lopsided. Tattered white roses tangled around each other like a briar patch along the front of the house.

Roses had been the only thing Alys had ever seen her mother take real care of, but, like everything else, they'd fallen out of favor and into neglect.

Alys couldn't look at the rose bushes without remembering the day they bloomed. It made her stomach churn. The man who'd sold the rose bushes had promised they would be *red*.

Her mother did not take disappointment gracefully.

They parked out front and stared at the house with a kind of grim apprehension.

Mary Ann thought it looked like it would collapse in on itself if she breathed too hard. She looked at the other girl beside her, and the way every muscle in her body seemed to tense. Despite the fact that she'd never lived anywhere else, Alys didn't call this place home. She'd find no comfort being there. "Can I use your phone?"

Alys looked at her.

"So I can call for a ride."

"Oh…yeah, of course." Alys fished her cell phone from her pocket. No bars. While a cell phone was handy to have anywhere else, unless you were on Main Street, you couldn't call the reception dependable in Appleweed. She sighed and climbed out of the car. "We'll have to go inside."

While the house itself incited contempt from its youngest resident, the steps leading up to it had a much different emotional attachment. Alys couldn't argue that they weren't cold, decaying, and uneven—by physical merit alone they had no virtues over the house itself. But they did have good memories. They had been a place free from any parents, and Alys and Charlie had spent countless hours on them.

"You okay?" Mary Ann nudged her, and Alys realized she'd just been loitering at the foot of the stairs.

"He was sitting there. Just yesterday." Alys chewed her bottom lip and fingered the note in her pocket. "Playing chess."

"Oh."

Alys stared hard at the stairs one moment longer. She thought over their last interaction and desperately rummaged through the smallest details. There had to have been signs. Something she missed. Something that would have helped prevent it if only she'd noticed.

He hadn't mentioned the fight with his father that morning. He always told her about them. It was how they kept each other sane. How had she not noticed he was keeping that from her?

Alys shook off the heavy feeling in her chest and started up the steps. She opened the door as if pulling too hard would not only yank it from the hinges, but also bring the entire house down on top of them.

The interior was dark and musty, and the air a bitter cocktail of one-part oxygen, two-parts vodka, and cigarette smoke.

Mary Ann coughed.

"Sorry. Try to hold your breath."

Mary Ann covered her nose and mouth with her sleeve. She was about to ask why Alys was being so quiet and secretive in her own house when the answer presented itself.

Sitting in the far corner of the living room was Alys's mother. Lucy Carroll might have been a beautiful woman at one point, but years in Appleweed had turned her as sour as the inedible crabapples that the town was named after. A fresh cigarette was balanced between her fingers as she pored over a magazine. A glass of what pretended to be ice water rested half consumed on the table beside her. She looked up and scowled. "Who's this?"

"Mary Ann Bosk. Susanne's kid. She works with me at the diner." Alys spoke in a very precise, albeit cautious tone, as if addressing an interrogator.

"Oh, yeah? What happened to that little fag you're always hanging around?"

Mary Ann's eyes darted to Alys, whose stare didn't so much as falter from her mother's.

"You can use the phone in my room." Alys inclined her head to indicate that Mary Ann should follow.

"Shouldn't you be at work?" Lucy leaned forward in her chair to gaze after them and grab her glass of "water".

"Shouldn't you be sober?" Alys closed her bedroom door behind them.

Mary Ann noticed the way Alys locked the multiple latches on the door: methodical, as if by pure muscle memory and habit. "You talk to your mother like that?"

"Believe me, she's done worse." Alys moved to the bedside table. "I guess I should be grateful. I might not have met Charlie had she been a better person." She picked up the cordless telephone and held it out to the other girl.

"Do you want to talk about it?"

Alys's extended arm went slack and her eyes looked towards the far end of the room. "No."

"I'm a good listener."

"Well, I'm not a good talker." Alys slumped onto the bed, thought about it more, and shrugged. "I wouldn't know what to say.

Something like I can't believe it, or how it doesn't seem real?" She looked at the phone still cradled in her hand, and her thumb mimicked the pattern of dialing Charlie's number over and over again. "It *doesn't* seem real," she admitted. "Maybe it will never seem real. It's funny, because I don't even want to cry about it now. I don't…feel much of anything about it now. It's just another nightmare I'll eventually wake up from… I mean, I *know* I'm going to wake up from this, because there's no way he can actually be *gone*." Her focus softened and she reached into her pocket to feel Charlie's note again. "I must sound crazy to you."

Mary Ann shook her head.

"It's just…he's always been here, and now he's not. And…I'm not sure where that leaves me."

"What do you mean?"

"We had all these plans, you know? Once we'd saved up enough…we were going to get out of here. I didn't much care where, as long as it wasn't here, but Charlie…Charlie had his heart set on Seattle." Alys smiled, her mind far away from the present situation in her bedroom.

"You couldn't shut him up about it. You'd think it was the Promised Land, the way he went on…a city full of culture and art and opportunity…such a ridiculously idealistic perspective of the place, really."

"Were you in love with him?"

"What?" Alys's head snapped around to look at her.

Mary Ann shrank back a little towards the door.

"No." She let the word stand on its own before continuing. "It wasn't like that, he…" She took a deep breath and replaced the phone on the cradle. "I don't know. Maybe I loved him…but it doesn't matter now, does it?"

Mary Ann nodded and looked away, debating on asking the question that etiquette insisted remain unspoken but curiosity longed to ask. "Do you know why he did it?"

Alys shook her head, her eyes stinging again. "I don't know. I know he was having a hard time. I know he was on new medication. I know he wasn't happy with his therapist, and I know his father was still the abusive asshole he'd always been, but…" She rested her head in her hands. "I didn't see this coming."

Mary Ann sat down on the bed beside her. "How could you?"

"I was his best friend. *It's my job to know.*"

"This isn't your fault."

"Isn't it?"

"No."

The conversation hit an uncomfortable dead end with neither party feeling convinced by the other.

Mary Ann picked up a picture frame that had been sitting on the bedside table by the phone. "This is him, right?"

Alys looked up from her hands, her eyes red but dry. "Yeah." She took the picture from Mary Ann and ran her fingers over the glass and frame with a fond smile. "We'd driven up to Seattle last summer—told his parents we were college scouting."

The photo had been taken just outside of Pike Place Market, around the golden pig statue in true tourist fashion. Alys was pretending to ride the pig while Charlie stood to her left, donning his best "I'm lost" expression as he held a map upside down.

"Who's the boy on the right? He looks familiar."

Alys's eyes rested on another handsome face that she'd almost forgotten. Dark spiky hair, freckled, and a grin like a madman. Black rimmed glasses rested low on a strong nose as he mimed stroking a beard that would never grow. She breathed a laugh. "Brian. Brian Mercer. He graduated two years before us."

"Oh, yeah. I didn't know you two knew each other."

Alys nodded. "Yeah, he and Charlie are— *were*…shit." She stopped. "He won't have heard."

"Heard what?"

"About Charlie. No one would have told him."

Mary Ann shifted uncomfortably. "Are you sure?"

"Well, yeah—I mean—no one knew he and Charlie were together but me."

"Oh." Mary Ann blushed.

Alys shuffled through the phone numbers in her cell phone and took the cordless off the cradle again. She hesitated and then set the receiver back down again.

"What's wrong?"

"I can't do this over the phone. He shouldn't hear like that."

"Then what are you going to do? Drive up to Seattle?"

Alys took this as a serious suggestion, and nodded. "Yeah. I think that's for the best." She dropped to the floor and slid a suitcase out from under the bed.

"Okay, um…I can cover your shifts till you get back." It was the only helpful thing Mary Ann could think of to offer. "I think we can spare you for a few days — maybe even a week. If I ask Mom."

Alys paused in her search through her closet. She could afford a week. She could afford a hell of a lot more than a week. They had been waiting until the end of the summer to leave for good, but that had been for his sake. She had enough right now. "I don't think I'm coming back." She grabbed an armful of clothing and dumped it into the suitcase.

"What?" Mary Ann squeaked.

"I mean I'm going. I'm finally getting out of this hellhole and I'm not looking back."

Mary Ann's eyes darted about for argumentative reasoning. "But you can't."

"Why not? I've got the money. Charlie's gone. I've literally no reason to stay anymore."

"What about your mom?"

"You met her."

"Yes, but—but—" Mary Ann could feel the anxiety of not knowing what to say in a situation where things demanded to be said rising in her throat.

"But who will she steal liquor money from?" Alys continued her hurried packing. Only the important things went. She grabbed the picture from the bedside table, necessary clothes. Shoes. Every form of identification she had. "But who will pay the mortgage? But who will she blame for all of her problems?"

Mary Ann clammed up.

"But *what*, Mary Ann?"

"She's your mother."

"I think that word means something else to you."

"My mom's pretty difficult to deal with too, but—"

"No," Alys laughed. "Mary Ann, your mom may be a hard-ass and all, but she is nothing like Lucy. Susanne loves the stuffing out of you. She may be a little over-dedicated to her restaurant, but if ever the day came between picking between the two of you, she'd choose you in a heartbeat."

"I'm not so sure."

"No," Alys insisted, grabbing Mary Ann by the arm. "Listen. That woman out there, half-drowned on rubbing alcohol? She'd sell me for a little extra cash if she were sober enough to figure out what market to talk to."

"I don't think—"

"When I was a kid, I wore nothing but long sleeves to cover the bruises on my arms. I've had nightmares about her since before I can even remember. I bought a bolt for my door when I was ten because she started bringing her boyfriends home. Do you understand?"

Mary Ann nodded, wide-eyed. "I'm sorry."

"I'm not telling you so you'll feel sorry for me. I'm telling you so you understand why I'm doing this," Alys answered, releasing her arm.

Mary Ann looked around the room, gradually regaining her composure. "How can I help?"

An hour or two had passed when Alys peeked out of her room. The smell of smoke had gone stale. "I think she went to bed," she whispered.

"It's barely noon!"

Alys looked at her with a raised eyebrow. "Right."

The two crept from the room, Mary Ann's arms full of pillows and blankets, while Alys slung a backpack over one shoulder, and toted a wheeled suitcase behind her.

The house was still, and every creak in the floor made them pause.

"Wait." Mary Ann stopped as Alys reached for the front door and looked back at the empty and decrepit living room. "Shouldn't you leave a note?"

"And say what?"

Mary Ann shrugged. "Goodbye?"

"More like good riddance."

Mary Ann gave her a look.

Alys exhaled through her teeth in frustration, the air causing the hair around her face to blow up. "Fine. I'll write a note." She opened the door and held out her car keys to Mary Ann. "Start loading the car."

Mary Ann made the awkward descent down the crooked steps, peeking over the marshmallow fluff of bedding in her arms. She stumbled her way to the car and unloaded her arms in the back seat before Alys was out the front door and down the stairs herself. "That was fast," she remarked.

"We're not really a long goodbye kind of family," came the flat reply.

"But you did write a note?" Mary Ann opened the door for Alys to put in both the suitcase and backpack.

"*Yes, I wrote a note.*" Alys tossed her items in and held her hand out for the car keys.

Mary Ann hesitated. "What did it say?"

Alys exhaled through her teeth again and wiggled her fingers insistently. "The only thing I could have thought that she'd care about. Gimme."

Satisfied, Mary Ann handed her the keys and they both climbed into the car once more.

"You sure you want me to drop you back off at work?"

"Yeah, Mom certainly can't manage all day two waitresses short."

Alys glanced sideways at her. "Are you mad at me for leaving?"

"No. If anything, I'm a little jealous." Mary Ann paled a little and tried to clarify. "Not that it's—I mean what happened—I'm not saying—"

"*Breathe*."

"I just meant…I wish I could leave."

"You could."

"Maybe." Mary Ann shrugged. "One day. When I'm not needed at the restaurant anymore."

"Pretty vague date."

"Hopelessly vague," Mary Ann said. "But it means the world to my mom, you know? When I leave, it'll be the only thing she'll have to keep her company. So…I just want to be sure…that everything will be okay without me."

Alys smiled as they pulled up to the diner, looking at the girl she'd shared both classes and shifts with since junior high. "I'm sorry we never really talked until today. I think we might have been friends."

Mary Ann gave a tiny but honest smile. "I don't see why we can't still be."

"You do have my number in the roster," Alys said.

"Have a safe trip, okay?"

She nodded.

Mary Ann slid out of the passenger seat with a wave. "Goodbye, Alyson."

It would be her only send off before she took to the highway, the diner, the swamp, and Charlie's house vanishing to a pinpoint behind her. The town itself didn't change much from her departure. No tears were shed, no memories fondly recalled. Both Karen and Charles Lewis would notice her absence at the funeral, but neither would mention it. Appleweed remained much as it ever had: grey and still.

The only real thing Alyson Carroll left in her wake was a note. Much like the one Charlie left her, it was a simple, uninspired note that the recipient would spend the next few days reading before she understood it. A note that read:

You can sell it all. I'm not coming back for it.

Chapter 5

WORLDS COLLIDE

Alys had been driving for a while when the storm finally hit. Rain gushed from the heavens as the little Jetta clung to the stunted highway, winding through the valley towards greater highways that would take her above sea level. The car was sputtering more than usual, as if trying to cough up the water that was starting to flood some of the deeper dips in the road.

Alys took very little notice of the rain. She was determined to plow through it to her destination. Her eyes flickered to the watch on her wrist. An hour. Maybe more. The odometer on the car had been broken when she bought it, but by time alone, she had to be at least sixty miles from Appleweed.

Everything seemed so much more color-ful this far out—even when she looked at it through the half-inch of rain that slid off her windshield. In Appleweed, it was as if every-thing faded under the sheer amount of precip-itation like a shirt that had gone through the wash too many times.

In theory, Appleweed was home, in that Alys had never lived anywhere else. She was born there, and the town would have been content to let her die there, as well. That's what most people did. Some would travel, but most would just trudge through the day without any other thought of the world out-side. Life in Appleweed was too exhausted to notice its own malcontent.

She was finally getting away from all that, finally pulling herself out from under the heavy cloud. But she was doing it alone.

Alys shook her head. "Why didn't he just wait?"

It wasn't going to be long. They could have left together. They could have left *last night*, if he'd wanted. It would have been financially tight, but surely they'd have been able to work something out—something better than *that*.

Something white reflected back the glare of the headlights, and her attention refocused on the last thing a driver wants to see.

Someone stood in the middle of the road.

She swerved the car to the right—a knee-jerk instinct that, in any other weather, might not have been so foolish. But the tires spun out over large puddles and she felt the car ram into the guard rail, which broke under its weight and velocity. The airbags deployed and the world was silent.

The car slid down the steep hill, and her hand flailed for the emergency break. It was a fruitless effort. The tires were too old and worn to gain any traction on the wet grass, and so it continued down the embankment unhindered. The car bucked as it passed over some kind of bump that scraped the underside of the car—something metal, something sharp. It was enough to pop the back right tire, but not enough to slow the car, only make it spin uncontrollably. A terrifying adaptation of a carnival tilt-a-whirl ride.

Alys closed her eyes against her growing nausea.

The car's pirouettes came to an abrupt halt as it slammed into some kind of rock face at the bottom, causing Alys to fall forward on the already deflating airbag.

***

Alys opened her eyes, her head pounding. She coughed and sat back, every muscle in her body protesting the movement. The dust from the airbags had settled. How long had she been out?

Her now broken wristwatch had no answer, and so she discarded it on the seat beside her.

She pinched her nose out of precaution, feeling for a break of any kind. It seemed okay. She slid her hand farther up, feeling her forehead. That did not feel okay. It burned and stung even when she wasn't touching it.

Her heart was still racing.

Her fingers traced along her hairline, wiping away the cool moisture to examine it on her fingers. Sweat. Not blood.

She sighed in relief. She was lucky — more than lucky — she hadn't had a full frontal collision. She glanced at the rearview mirror, which reflected where the car made impact, but it was impossible to see anything through the spider web of cracks in the window.

Alys struggled with the car door, growling in frustration when it wouldn't budge. She pulled back and pressed herself against the door again, her knuckles turning white around the handle until it popped open like a champagne cork and she tumbled out. She closed her eyes, ice cold water sliding down her face. The grass squelched under her, far less solid after an hour of the rain.

The world wavered in a dance of downpour and disorientation. She blinked, trying to refocus her vision before untangling her limbs and clinging to the car frame for aid. Even in the thick veil of the rain, she could see where her car had broken through the guard rail up the hill. The grass was flattened in two lines which deepened into ruts in the mud as the trail drew closer and over a set of old railroad tracks. The tracks were slightly elevated, both wood and broken metal sticking up in a jagged fashion, as if someone had tried to uproot them and given up halfway through. That explained what had happened to her tire. She looked down, taking note of the thing that was now nothing more than a useless ripped ring of rubber that loosely draped over the hubcap. She winced and moved around to look at the back of the car, crumpled and collapsed like a soda can.

"Fuck." She reached into her car and dug out her cell phone.

No service.

Of course.

She threw it back into the car and turned back towards the rock face, which, now that she had a good look at it, was not a rock face at all. It was a train tunnel. Old. Older than she would have thought possible. Like the tracks that ran through it, it was falling apart, and had been devoid of any human contact for quite some time. The brick was discolored and splotchy, weathered from both rain and sun. Moss, along with some sort of ivy, had long since taken over and could have been the only thing holding the stones in place.

Still, it'd be dry.

Alys wiped the front of her shirt, intending to remove some of the mud and water, but it just smudged. She grumbled and climbed back into the car to grab her backpack. She picked up the phone again as a second thought.

Her joints hurt. Some part of her knew that wasn't a great sign, but she dismissed that thought with the assurance that she didn't need an ambulance.

She tried to slam the door shut behind her and trudged towards the tunnel's cover. Once the storm cleared, she'd flag down a car for a ride into Seattle — or, at least walk enough distance to get service on her phone.

The inside of the tunnel was dusty, but otherwise surprisingly clean for something that had been abandoned for so long. She used her phone as a flashlight, peering into the depths. It seemed to be empty. No other stranded travelers, and it seemed to be devoid of any visible creepy-crawlies.

She checked her pocket for Charlie's note, relieved to see it was still there and had miraculously been spared from the rain.

Alys pulled dry clothes from her backpack, piling them on top of the bag itself to keep them clean. The note was safely transferred to the pocket of a dry blue-hooded sweatshirt before she attended to her wet clothes. Her fingers were numb and struggled with buttons and zippers, which just added to her frustration. She peeled the wet shirt off and flailed a little at the end to get it off. She wrung it out before using it to attempt to dab the remaining moisture off her skin before pulling a clean white top over her head.

It was at that moment that Alys realized she was not as alone as she had first thought.

He was standing at the mouth of the tunnel, obscured by the dim sunlight that had managed to break through the clouds and rain.

They both stood frozen in the moment, not thirty feet apart, unsure what to do with each other, eyes locked.

The wet shirt in Alys's hand dripped onto her foot with a faint *plop* as it hit the toe of her shoe. Her face flushed as she remembered what she had been doing moments before this stranger's arrival. "*How long have you been there?*"

Even in the poor light, she could see he was taken aback. "Excuse me?"

"You, standing there, how long?"

"Are you talking to me?"

"You see anyone else in this tunnel?"

He actually bothered to look about. "No," he remarked, seemingly amazed. "I...I don't..." His eyes scanned about the entrance. "Remarkable... "

"*What* is?"

He shook his head. "Nothing. I guess...I didn't expect anyone else to be here."

"Did you see anything?"

"See anything?"

Alys pointedly wrung out the wet shirt again.

He swallowed. "No." He wandered farther into the tunnel.

"Stop."

"What?"

"Don't come any closer."

He stopped, bewildered. "Are you... afraid of me?"

Her eyes had adapted to the dark, and now that he was closer, she could see him a bit more clearly. He was different looking. She'd never seen silver-white hair on anyone who looked so young. He must have had a fantastic stylist. It contrasted against the dark copper hue of his skin. His was a handsome appearance, if not a little striking. As for his clothing? It was muddy, much like hers, but beneath the dirt, she could tell the fabric was very fine—even if they did look like pajamas. "I'm not afraid of anything." It was a blatant lie, but it at least sounded convincing.

"My name is Oswin." He smiled and extended his hand.

There was a softness to his smile that was irritatingly infectious. So, instead of returning it, she handed him the wet shirt to hold as she retrieved the sweatshirt to cover her bare shoulders. "Mary Ann." Two lies in less than two minutes. Her mother had to be rubbing off on her.

"Mary Ann." Oswin shook his head a little. He seemed simultaneously in disbelief and impressed with something about their meeting, but he wasn't being forthcoming about why. "I'm sorry…if I startled you."

"S'ok," Alys said. "Would you mind…?" She made a turning motion with her finger.

"Of course." Oswin turned his back to her. He realized he was still holding the wet shirt, but there was no place to put it.

With some semblance of privacy, Alys began to change her pants.

"I saw the crash," Oswin murmured. He heard a pause in the ruffling of fabric. "I wanted to make sure you were all right."

Silence.

"*Are you*...all right?"

Alys resumed changing. "I'm fine."

"Good." He sounded relieved. "And your...um...vehicle?"

"My *car*?" Alys re-laced her sneakers and laughed. "It's great. Just great. The tire's blown, the glass is shattered, the engine is leaking fluid all over the ground, but I'm sure it's going to pull through."

"Really?"

"Of course not," Alys snapped, leaning around him to snatch the shirt from his hands. "It's totaled. Oversized paperweight. Surprised you didn't see it. It's just outside."

"I did," Oswin said, turning around. "But I don't...I was just trying to be polite."

"Well, I don't need polite. I need my car to work." Alys crouched by her bag as she packed things back into it, her face softening a little with guilt. "I'm sorry. I'm not usually like this. At least, not to total strangers."

"You're under a lot of stress."

"You have no idea…" She looked up at him. "Would you mind giving me a lift to the nearest town? My phone doesn't get any service out this far."

"A lift?"

"A ride," she said. "You know…in your *car*?"

"Oh!" Oswin awed in understanding. "I don't have a car."

Alys's shoulders slumped in disappointment. "You don't have a car?"

He shook his head.

"Then…what are you doing this far out of town without a car?"

"Well…"

Alys rose quickly, pointing an accusing finger. "You're the idiot I nearly hit, aren't you?"

Oswin backed away. "Actually —"

"What were you *thinking*, standing in the middle of the road? You could have been killed!" The memory of the crash flooded into her mind, her heart beginning to race again. The cold terror sent a burning hot anger to her face. "*I* could have been killed!"

Oswin raised his hands. "Forgive me. I

didn't realize that you'd—I'm not from—I didn't think that I'd…at least you're okay?"

"I'm not okay. I'm stranded! Because of you!" Alys let out a growl of frustration that echoed down the tunnel. She kicked the wall, fuming.

A tense silence settled between them as she turned around to face him again, but it didn't last. There was a calming dream-like quality to his presence and as they looked at each other, Alys's breathing eased from a heavy rise and fall to a light and relaxed rhythm.

Alys tore her gaze away, trying to cling to an unwelcoming scowl. "Why are you out here, anyway?"

"Waiting for someone," Oswin said.

"In the middle of the road?"

"In here, actually." He gestured vaguely to the interior of the tunnel.

Alys's nose wrinkled. "Kinda a weird place to meet someone, isn't it?"

Oswin's mouth twitched into a smile. "Yes…I suppose it is."

She paused. "Could *they* give me a ride?"

A laugh erupted out of Oswin, and he shook his head. "No."

Alys glared.

He swallowed hard and his eyes flickered to the floor. "I just mean…I doubt we're going in the direction you need us to."

"Oh."

A silence fell between them again, and Oswin reached into his pocket and produced a gleaming gold pocket watch. It flicked open. It was simple in its outward design, but possessed a certain mythic quality about it.

Alys found herself staring, drawn to it. "Are you late?"

"What?" Oswin snapped the watch closed.

"You look worried."

"Oh." He glanced back at the watch. "No. I'm on time. They're late."

"Your friends?"

"Yes."

Yet another awkward pause.

"You don't see those very often."

"Which?"

"*Watch*." Alys smiled and pointed at his pocket watch. "You don't see those very often."

"It was a gift from my mother." He seemed

a little charmed by her interest. "Would you like to see it?"

Alys's eyes widened, and the corners of her mouth twitched up involuntarily into a surprised smile. "Seriously?"

Oswin laughed and offered it to her.

Alys accepted it with caution, as if she expected it to bite her. She cradled the watch in the cup of her palm, the chain dangling between her fingers. She raised her free hand and traced her fingertips over the design etched into the gold, flourishing outward in a petal-like fashion. It looked like some kind of bloom, but not one she recognized. "What kind of flower is this?"

"It's a reference to a poem by Samuel Taylor Coleridge."

"What poem?" Alys looked back at him, her eyebrows raised with interest.

Oswin recited from memory, "'What if you slept, And what if, In your sleep, You dreamed, And what if, In your dream, You went to heaven, And there plucked a strange and beautiful flower, And what if, When you awoke, You had that flower in your hand, Ah, what then?'"

"Beautiful," Alys said, turning her full attention back to the watch.

"Very." Oswin observed her with the same curiosity she was exhibiting for the watch in her palm.

"Any reason why, or did your mother just like the poem?"

"Oh, she wasn't the one who had the flower engraved. It was given to her after... well..." Oswin shrugged. "It just seemed to fit, I guess."

Alys released the spring latch and startled at the movement inside until she realized it was her own reflection. The lid held a mirror. She laughed, embarrassed, and scrutinized her appearance. "I look like a drowned rat."

"Hardly," Oswin assured her.

"Says the other drowned rat," Alys commented wryly. Her focus shifted to the watch face. Delicate hands: an hour, a minute, a second, and another? "Your clock has too many hands," she murmured.

"It has the amount it needs."

"What's this fourth one?" Alys brought it up to her face to examine it closer. She noticed it moved. Not in accordance with some kind of time change, but, rather, so it could point towards the opposite wall of the tunnel. "Oh! It's a compass." She brought it down again and turned towards the wall, watching the hand point forward now. "So that's north."

"Sure," Oswin said with a wide smile.

Alys looked at him, puzzled by his answer, but then heard the whistle.

It was muffled perhaps, and somewhere in the distance, but it was, without a doubt a train whistle.

Alys's hand tensed, closing the watch. "Did you hear that?"

"No." Oswin looked nervous.

Again, the whistle sounded, louder this time.

Alys's eyes widened. "There! There it is again. It sounds like a train. Tell me you heard that."

"Y-yes."

Alys crouched to get her bag, but stopped. "But…it can't be a train. I saw the tracks myself, and they're in no condition to have anything travel on—"

Near the mouth of the tunnel, from out of the brick wall itself, like some kind of dream between sleeping and waking, came a beautiful, glistening white engine. It turned to line up on the tracks, and though she knew it had to be speeding towards them, it seemed to slow to a graceful waltz rather than the quick, stampeding tango she'd imagined a train's pace to be.

Oswin grabbed her and pulled her up against the wall, flattening her form against it with his own.

Alys's eyes squinted shut, anticipating impact or the rushing of a great wind to pass by them. Neither happened. She peeked over Oswin's shoulder and saw the train had, in fact, stopped neatly in front of them.

It was designed for no less than royalty, to be sure. Beautiful architecture, crafted alabaster and gold, and despite the messy business you'd imagine trains to be involved in, it was spotless.

Oswin released her and took a careful step back. "I'm afraid I have to go now."

"This is your ride?" Alys looked from him to the train and back again, her voice quiet and hoarse with disbelief.

Oswin smiled but gave her no direct answer. He took her hand in both of his and kissed her knuckles. "It's been a pleasure, Mary Ann."

Alys could only blink in reply.

He climbed onboard the train but paused to look back at her one last time, shaking his head, still amazed at something he refused to vocalize. "Perhaps I'll see you in your dreams."

It was a strange goodbye. The words suggested some sort of cheesy, flirtatious sentiment, but there was something in his tone of voice, some kind of simple sincerity, like he'd suggested he'd see her around the neighborhood.

The door closed behind him and the train eased backward a moment before sliding forward again, like a ballerina preparing for a great leap into the air. Its surreal grace was almost soundless.

Alys watched as it moved past her, the rush causing her hair to whip around her face. It didn't go far, perhaps only a few meters, before turning back towards the wall it had first emerged from, vanishing through the brick once more as if it were no more solid than fog.

It took her a moment to regain herself. Her mouth opened and then closed, having formulated something to say, but now she realized there was no longer anyone to hear it. She moved across the tunnel to where the train had vanished through the brick. She raised her palm and pressed it firmly against the surface. It felt solid enough. She moved a little farther down and rammed it with her shoulder. Still nothing—except a bruised arm and shoulder. Not quite satisfied, she leaned on the wall with her hand, moving slowly down the tunnel just to confirm with her senses that there was no possible way a *train,* of all things, could just—Alys fell through the wall.

Chapter 6

DREAMERS

Oswin leaned against the closed door to catch his breath. He glanced over his shoulder and out the train window, watching the brick pass by in a blur.

Humans, as far as he could recollect, did not — because they could not — see his kind. At least not while waking. They were incapable of it. The living could not stray into their world beyond dreaming, just as Dreams could not enter the physical realm completely. The only people capable of traversing between the two as they pleased were, and had always been, the Fae.

Now *there* was an idea.

Oswin stepped farther in and opened the door to the passenger car.

"Ah, Your Highness." The Queen's Reason was a thin man of dark complexion, sharply dressed in the finest fashion Terra Mirum could offer. He removed his top hat, stooping into a low bow and up again. "It is a relief to see you safe."

"Basir." Oswin clasped the other gentleman's forearm, relieved to see a familiar face. His eyes scanned the rest of the car, but they appeared to be the only occupants. "I was hoping I might have a word with Robin, actually."

Before joining the Court of Dreams, Robin had served the royal houses of Arden, who were more than infamous for their dalliances with mortals and their realm. The Coleridge Clock itself, was an artifact of the complex history between Fae and mortal. If anyone could shed light on why the human had been able to see him, it would be her.

Oswin looked down at himself, remembering he was still wearing his pajamas. "And perhaps a change of clothing."

"Yes, of course. There are fresh clothes waiting for you in your room." Basir gestured towards the doors that led to the other cars. "But you will find Robin in the engine with her brother, making sure he does not crash this blasted thing."

That was unlucky. Where Robin could be counted on for discretion, Jack would let any information slip at a sip of ale.

"I suppose it will have to wait."

"Is it something that I can help with?" As the Queen's Reason, Basir was a living fount of facts and figures. He could recount statistics and mathematical figures off the top of his head, explain complex scientific theories, and even name every species of insect, if the situation called for it.

"Perhaps," Oswin said. It didn't seem entirely unlikely that Basir would know. "I was just wondering if…" He paused, and his mouth contorted as he wondered how to introduce such a question. "I mean, has it ever been known…?" He took a deep breath and tried again. "Is it possible, even remotely, for a human to see us?"

"Of course," Basir said. "Their minds often trespass through the veil between our worlds. In sleep, of course, they have always wandered among us—though rarely out of the Tulgey Wood."

Oswin picked nervously at his nails. "What about when we've wandered into their world?"

"There have been a few accounts of conversations with their kind when their subconscious has one leg in their world and one in ours," Basir said. "It is a messy business. I confess, I have not quite figured out the science of it. Robin would have me believe there is none. Preposterous."

"What about when they *are* fully conscious?"

"It could not happen."

"It *did* happen."

Silence overtook the passenger car.

"Sire…" To his credit, Basir was trying to not sound patronizing, but he was failing. "Are you sure — ?"

"I met someone," Oswin insisted firmly. "She saw me — *spoke* to me, and I don't mean she spoke and it just happened to be in my direction. We held a conversation. I was able to touch her as if she and I were no different from one another." He reached out to the wall of the train car. "She saw the train. Undoubtedly, she saw us leave through the wall. For all I know, she could have followed us."

"Followed us?" Basir's posture seemed even stiffer than normal. "She could not have followed us, sire, truly, not if she's hu—"

"Dreamer," said a new voice.

Oswin and Basir startled as both men had assumed they were alone.

A lanky shadow of a man stood up at the far end of the car, seeming to glide into the aisle.

Oswin thought he must have been slumped down in the seat, considering the way his hair seemed even more tousled than normal. It would also explain why both of them had failed to notice him.

"Smoke." Basir did nothing to hide his disdain. "How long have you been just sitting there? Were you eavesdropping?"

"I was sleeping." Smoke had a way of toying with disapproval like a cat does with yarn. He strolled up the aisle to meet them, affecting a big stretch and yawn to further sell his defense. "Your voice carries,. It would have required a great effort on my part to stop from hearing."

"One I'm sure you did not even attempt."

"You don't make a living by *not* hearing things, my lord." Smoke flashed a wide grin and gently patted Basir's cheek. Without even a hint of apology, Smoke turned away from Basir to face only Oswin as if he'd been an active part of the conversation the entire time. "This girl you met—she's a Dreamer."

Neither Oswin nor Basir gained much understanding from this piece of information, so Smoke elaborated.

"There are few of mortal birth born with a particular gift: They see beyond the veil between our worlds, which allows them to interact with us much like they do each other. It's rare, but not unheard of. In the human world, it's usually dismissed as an over-active imagination. Some use it as inspiration—becoming poets or artists—while others are convinced we are hallucinations and the poor souls end up in madhouses."

"How do you know all this?" Basir took a purposeful step back into Smoke's direct line of sight.

Smoke cocked his head to the side and grinned widely. "Please." He dismissed

Basir's question affectionately, adjusting his collar. "You said she may have followed you?" Smoke focused on Oswin, which suggested the prince was under interrogation.

Oswin nodded, unable to remember if he'd ever seen Smoke look so serious. "The train, yes, it's possible, but I don't know—"

Smoke maneuvered between them towards the door.

"Where are you going?"

"To look for her," Smoke said. "We can't have a human just wandering aimlessly about with a Nightmare on the throne. What if she's seen? What if she's *caught*?"

"What are *you* going to do?" Oswin's brow furrowed.

Smoke's mouth settled into the same wide and cryptic grin that came so naturally to his face. He looked over his shoulder, sizing up Prince and Reason with eyes that respected neither, and said, "Whatever has to be done."

***

Alys was falling.

She had been falling for quite some time

now. She hit nothing and she saw nothing, just continued to fall down an endless black tunnel until falling felt an awful lot like floating. Sure enough, Alys was drifting down what she could only identify as a brick tunnel, bare of any notable details save for a black iron staircase that clung to the bricks and wound down into the dark.

She flailed her limbs. Swimming was a skill all of the children in Appleweed were taught, but few very rarely used it thereafter. The stroke Alys employed was befitting of the word--a manic mutilation of the dog-paddle. It was an awkward trip, but she did manage to reach the stairs. She gripped the rail and pulled herself over, slamming her feet down to ground herself.

At least, with stairs, she could decide her own pace. Falling, despite how little effort it required, was rather exhausting.

By all logic, it should have been dark. She shouldn't have been able to see anything at all, but, somehow, her eyes made out the details of the stairs and the tunnel around her as if a small lantern or spotlight followed her movements.

She leaned on the rail and gave the great distance above her a look. Though she knew it existed, she couldn't see the top where her fall had begun, and when she looked down, she couldn't see where the fall would have ended, either.

"The hell...?" Her voice echoed in both directions through the tunnel. "This goes on forever."

Her eyes closed. Things had been well within the bounds of reality until that man showed up. Her lips pursed. Falling through walls, great white trains, and strange men with pocket watches. Her head was starting to hurt again.

There had to be a logical explanation.

Her mind picked through recent events like old photographs, examining the evidence and investigating every detail for meaning. She'd been driving — wide awake, albeit distracted. Thinking about *Charlie*.

She did not allow herself to linger on that.

Which is *why* she didn't see the man, Oswin, in the middle of the road until it was too late. She had swerved, hit the guardrail, and —

Crashed.

Her eyes snapped open, and flashes of twisted, crumpled metal pushed their way into her focus until she could see nothing else. Her head burned from the memory, and she raised a hand to touch it. It hadn't felt too terrible, but what if...

Alys shivered, uncomfortable with the conclusions her own mind was drawing, and started down the stairs. It was movement for the sake of movement more than anything else--a distraction, not a direction, though moving down, if she actually thought about it, made more sense than up. Going up meant sitting in a cold, wet cave by herself.

Down held the potential for anything.

The scenery was monotonous and ugly—old brick no matter where you looked. Only the black iron staircase broke up the chalky red patchwork pattern. She placed one hand on the wall, letting her fingers glide over the brick to feel the rough texture against her skin.

"If I'm dead, this is a shit afterlife," Alys said to no one.

It wasn't an implausible idea that this place was some kind of personal purgatory. She'd never been religious, so she wasn't the best judge on what could or couldn't pass as an eternal waiting room, but endless stairs seemed to fit in that category. Still, since she'd never received any kind of religious education, that had to count for something, right? Was ignorance considered a legitimate excuse in heaven?

The more Alys thought about what it meant to be dead, the more her head hurt, and the more her head hurt, the more she began to believe that she was, in fact, *not dead* at all.

"I really hope I'm not in a coma..."

Her palm tickled as she ran her hand over something new. She stopped and looked to see small patches of ivy that had climbed up the wall to that very point. She blinked and her gaze followed the wall, seeing the ivy peek up more and more as the stairs twisted downward. She moved to lean out over the rail, squinting through the dim light. The vegetation looked to be getting thicker the lower she descended. It had to be emerging from somewhere.

Her heart skipped a beat.

She saw a faint change—a slight outline altering the uniformity of the darkness—that,

somehow, because she had not been looking for it, was all the easier to see. Her eyes
focused hard on the suggestion of a shape.

It was not her imagination, and it was
not a trick of the light. It was a door. A small,
unimpressive door set into the wall in such
a way that you'd almost miss it, but it was a
door, nevertheless. It also appeared to be only
a few flights down from where she stood.

Alys pushed herself off the rail and down
the stairs, taking them two at a time. Down
and down and down again, she rounded the
spiral so quickly she felt dizzy.

And then the stairs ended.

Her hands caught the railing at first, but
momentum still took her halfway over it.
The railing dug into her stomach and her feet
momentarily lost touch with the ground as
she teetered forward like a child balancing
on monkey bars. She stared into the darkness of the tunnel that continued downwards
and gulped.

The train must have continued on down that way.

Alys righted herself slowly and tried to
regain the breath the railing had knocked out
of her while looking over her shoulder.

The door was plain and made of wood. In any other setting, it would have been ordinary, but in this place it was the only door within miles and miles of tunnel, and therefore, a novelty-- one that made her cautious as she approached it.

Her hand reached towards it, fingers fanning out before, one by one, they wrapped around the knob. She took a deep breath and turned her wrist to open it. It didn't move. Alys released the breath she hadn't realized she'd been holding. Locked. After all that, the door was locked. She chewed her bottom lip and dropped down to peer through the keyhole. This proved unhelpful. All she could see was a white marble tiled floor framed in black, and that was it. Just a floor—clean, very well-lit--but a floor just the same.

Alys rocked back on her heels and thought. As far as she could tell, there were two ways out of this tunnel. In reality, there were three ways out, but the third had a high risk of her falling to her death or getting run over by a train, so she didn't much consider it a valid option. Of the two options she did consider, she would either need to find a way through the door or she would have to walk all the way back up the stairs. Her eyes followed the route back up the ever-winding staircase.

One option.

Alys turned her full attention back on the door.

She pushed against it.

The wood had no give at all — it was solid.

She tapped her fingers on the surface.

"Hello?" said a voice from the other side. He sounded startled.

Alys blinked. It had never occurred to her to just *knock*. "Hello."

"Can I...?" The voice trailed off, seeming to evaluate the obscurity of the situation as if he was just as bewildered as Alys was to be there. "...help you?"

"Yes!" she said, feeling her excitement grow a little as the possibility of progress presented itself. "Yes, you can. I'm stuck in here."

"That sounds dreadful," said the voice.

"It is. It really is. Can you open the door?"

"Oh." The voice seemed to come to a kind of grim realization. "N-no."

Her face fell. "Why not?"

She heard him lean on the door and drop his voice to a whisper. "I'm not allowed."

"But how am I supposed to get out?"

"Are you to get out at all?" the voice whispered. "That's the first question, you know."

"Well…what else am I supposed to do?"

"Whatever you were doing, I suppose." There was a sudden finality to the voice, as if he'd decided he shouldn't be talking to anyone.

"I was trying to get in." Alys kicked the door.

"Look." She heard a rustle as if whoever was on the other side was pressing himself up against the door. He kept his voice down, but she could hear the tension when he spoke. "I'm really sorry I can't be of more help, but I have a job to do. Under no circumstance can I open this door because I'm on strict orders to not let anyone into the tunnel."

Alys's brows peaked. "But…I'm already in the tunnel."

He stopped cold. "Oh."

"Yeah."

"Oh, no…" His voice started to sound nervous—even panicky. "What should I do?"

"You'd better let me in."

"Y-yes." There was a jingling of keys, and the sound of one being jammed into the lock.

"Of course...of course." The door opened and a flood of light washed over her.

Alys blinked and walked inside, her eyes struggling to adjust. She heard the door close and lock behind her. She could see a black and white checker-board floor — marble, by the looks of it. It stretched down a hallway in front of her, lit by sunlight which poured in through large windows on the right side of the wall. She wondered how long she'd been in that tunnel, considering it had been pouring rain the last time she'd looked outside.

"Th-thank you," he said. The owner of the voice was a lanky sort of man with large, wide-set eyes. She couldn't tell if he was naturally pallid or if anxiety had drained him of all color. He reminded her of a frog, and would have looked rather unimpressive were he attired any differently. His uniform was a crisp black with white and silver trim. A strange gun was slung over one arm, long like a shotgun, but covered in intricate gears that led to the end of the barrel, which fanned out like a trumpet. He was some kind of soldier, of that, she had no doubt.

"No problem." She looked from him to the hallway, then to the gun. Where was she?

"L-look…i-if we could keep this between us…" he whispered.

"Of course," Alys said and looked down the hall. "How do I get outside?"

He pointed a shaking hand. "Down and to the right. *Don't* let the others see you were in here."

Alys felt her heart quicken. Her exact location was a little less relevant, as it was becoming more and more obvious that, regardless of where she was, she wasn't supposed to be here. She nodded her thanks, turned to leave, and stopped. "Don't you want to know how I got in there in the first place?"

The soldier looked sickened by the suggestion. "N-no." He shook his head and struck a regimented stance by the door. "I don't want to know a damned thing."

Chapter 7

DOUBT

"And then he left!" Basir had pulled Robin out of the engine room and to one of the private cars so he could relay the recent events. He was not an angry man, and the times he'd been seen to lose his temper were countable on one hand, but his rising frustration with Smoke's cryptic method of operation was palpable. "Just *left* without so much as an explanation of where he was going, what he would be doing, or if he planned on returning."

Robin was a small woman with spritely features. Her short hair was an outcropping of browns and reds with flecks of gold. It seemed to have a mind of its own by the way it swept over her eyes, flipped up at her cheekbones and chin, and spiked out at the base of her neck. Out of the windswept layers, small horns poked up around her temples, and long, pointed ears stuck out on either side of her head. Her skin had a translucent quality to it, catching the light with the faintest of shimmer. It was a quality many mortals had described as pixie dust. She leaned against the wall in front of the door. "It'll be fine, Basir."

"Fine? *Fine?*" he echoed, his volume increasing with each punctuated syllable. "The prince reports a human has somehow breached one of Terra Mirum's gates, breaking who knows how many laws of nature, a Nightmare is on the loose, and our only plan to remedy the situation is trusting that a changeling—"

"Basir," Robin warned.

"—will do whatever *has to be done,* and you call that fine? I do not know about you, but I am not reassured by that vague course of action. There are many words that could describe this situation, my dear Rhyme, but *fine* would not be one of them."

She sighed. "Smoke knows what he's doing."

"Really?" Basir folded his arms, leaning on the wall opposite of her. "Has a human ever trespassed into Terra Mirum before?"

"Well…" Robin averted her eyes. "No, not to my immediate knowledge."

"Has one even wandered into Arden before?"

"Not exactly *wandered*—"

"Has he, himself, been on the other side and walked among them?"

"I don't think so, but if you'd—"

"Then how, pray tell," Basir said, his voice rising ever so slightly in volume as it tended to when he was starting to panic, "could he possibly *know* what he is doing?"

"For starters, I think it's safe to say my crew and I know far better how to deal with humans in the physical realm than any citizen from your Kingdom. Furthermore, as a *changeling*, as you so politely put it, wouldn't he then be the most qualified out of any of us to handle this?"

Basir stopped, realizing the very obvious reason why Smoke knew so much about Dreamers. He was the product of one. He took a deep breath, realizing he'd far overstepped his bounds. "Robin, I was not trying to offend—"

"I realize his bloodline isn't the most traditional, but that doesn't mean he isn't loyal—that he isn't capable."

"That is not what I meant."

"You realize if we ever have a child, *that* is the same kind of prejudice it will have to contend with?"

The marriage between the late Queen's Rhyme and Reason had always been a controversial matter among the court. While it served as a great tribute to the peace between Dream and Fae, the kind of child such a union would bear had also stirred up considerable amounts of gossip in both kingdoms.

"It is not because of prejudice." Basir attempted to regain his calm before Robin lost hers.

"Oh, really?" she chuffed.

"Humans cannot exist in our world, Robin. Their control over the aether, or lack thereof, could be disastrous. It could destroy everything. Half-blood or not, Smoke could still pose that same threat."

"Oberon thought so, too," Robin sneered. "During the war, he was convinced that Smoke would be the key to tipping the scales in our favor. A Fae-born, who, much like his human father, could have possibly altered the reality around Terra Mirum as you know it." Her eyes narrowed. "Luckily for you, he was *wrong*."

Basir sighed. "I am sorry…I did not intend to start an argument about this."

"Why can't you just trust him?"

"Robin—"

"The war is long over, Basir. Smoke poses no threat to Dreams, and if it hadn't been for him, Oswin would have been executed. We never would have come this far."

"Yes, but—"

"Do you trust me?"

He stopped and met her eyes with a defeated frown. It was an unfair question, an unavoidable checkmate, particularly when employed in an argument with your spouse. He half-expected to see her trying to suppress a small but impishly triumphant grin. No such case. She was serious, and so he had to follow suit. "Intimately."

"Well, *I* trust *him*."

Basir's body grew slack, and he closed his eyes to ease his building anxiety. "I know.

I am...I am sorry. I just...I do not like not knowing what is going on." He tilted his head down, his forehead resting against her own.

"I know," she said.

"What does that even mean?" Basir didn't know if he was posing this question to his wife or the heavens. "'Whatever has to be done?'"

"Seems   pretty   self-explanatory." Robin shrugged.

"No, it seems ominous."

"Please don't start this again."

Basir pulled back, indignant. "I am not *starting* anything!" Their eyes met, and he lowered his voice again. "Robin, I am not trying to fight with you, truly. It was a genuine question. We have a Nightmare on the throne and a Dreamer roaming freely through the land. You know him. What did that mean? Take her back through the gate?"

"I don't know," Robin said. "Honestly, I don't think even he'll know until he finds her."

"He won't harm her, will he?" Oswin had just opened the door and heard the tail end of their conversation.

Both Robin and Basir startled like two parents caught fighting by one of their children. They looked at each other, the air tense with their inability to answer the question with full confidence.

"I don't see why it would ever have to come to that, Your Highness," Robin finally assured him. "He'll probably just take her back to the other side when he finds her. Far away from all of this so she can do no harm."

Oswin didn't look so convinced, yet nodded. It wasn't that he didn't trust Robin or her former colleagues, but before she'd taken her place in his mother's court as the King's Puck, she'd had more than her fair share of less than noble ways of taking care of things. He had no doubt they'd do whatever was most efficient in getting the job done. He just wasn't sure he was comfortable with what other consequences those kinds of methods might bring about.

They could feel the train beginning to slow, the ground catching up beneath them.

Oswin moved to look out the window, but all he saw was darkness. His brow furrowed. It was far too early to be night, so where were they? "Wait." He looked over his shoulder at the other two. "Why are we stopping here?"

"Because this is our stop?" Robin said, confused by his confusion.

Oswin's form tensed for one distrustful moment. The Nightmare had taken control of his guards and many others in the kingdom. Had she also taken control of his remaining allies in his absence? "This is not the home of my cousin." His voice was wary, and he noted all possible exits.

"Of course it isn't," Robin laughed, but neither Oswin nor Basir found the humor in the moment.

Basir rested a hand on his wife's shoulder and turned her towards the door to exit. "She means we travel on foot from here, Your Highness."

The door to the engine room slid open and a tall, impish sort of man emerged. Like his sister, Jack bore two horns and similarly pointed ears. Really, he and Robin could have been fraternal twins. The same unruly multi-colored hair, the same green eyes, and the same crooked smile.

"In case you hadn't noticed," Jack said, elaborating on Basir's far more polite explanation, rapping his knuckles against the wall.

98

"For all the speed this bitch has, she's got shit for stealth."

"Eloquent, Jack," Robin muttered as she passed by him to open the door to the outside and hop out. "You are a true poet among peasants."

"I speak the King's speech, same as you."

"Can't remember the last time I heard any King speak like that."

Oswin climbed from the car, looking around tentatively. "Where are we?"

"One of the caves just south of the Tulgey Wood," Basir answered, leaving the two siblings to bicker. "By the time they finally catch up to us and find the train, we'll be long gone."

"We're still about a mile or two out from Rosalind's." Oswin pursed his lips. They were running out of time.

Jack rolled his eyes. "Afraid you'll blister your royal feet?"

Robin elbowed him in the gut.

It was not enough to stop Basir from glaring in his direction. "Usurped or not, sirrah, this is still your future king. You will hold your tongue and afford him the respect that position demands."

Jack's face was the picture of mock alarm. "Oh, forgive me, Lord Reason, I meant no offense." And then the act was dropped as quickly as it had been created. "But that has never been my future King. Robin may have accepted this place as her home, but I have not. My loyalty is and will always be to Oberon." He didn't say traitor, per se, but the look he gave his sister and the tone of his voice left little to interpretation.

"And yet, when was the last time you stepped foot in Arden?" Robin asked flatly, not even slightly shaken by his accusations.

"I'm of Fae blood, sister. My heart may lead me to wander, but time does not erase that."

"It also doesn't erase debts or felonies."

"It doesn't matter," Oswin said, stopping them. "Regardless, wherever anyone's loyalties lie, they do not lie with the Nightmare, and that makes us allies with a common enemy. And that common enemy does not allow us the luxury of wasting our time bickering."

The two siblings looked at each other guiltily and Robin gave a sort of shrug, gesturing for her brother to lead the way out of the mouth of the tunnel.

Jack obliged, but in a manner that made it clear he was conceding to Oswin's logic, not his authority.

Oswin lengthened his strides until he was walking next to Robin and inclined his head so he could whisper, "He does know the war between Dream and Fae ended before I was even born, doesn't he?"

"Try not to take it personally," Robin apologized.

"Easier said than done."

"He volunteered to help me rescue you, so he can't really hate you so entirely," she said.

"Oh, good." Oswin forced a smile. "That's a comfort."

"It's a matter of pride," she continued quietly. "Our kingdoms may be at peace, but there are some who weren't very pleased with how the war ended. Most of them soldiers."

Oswin frowned.

"It's nothing personal, Your Highness. Jack was one of us who hungered for victory. Instead, he got a treaty, and, for a soldier, there's hardly any glory in that." Robin sighed and shrugged. "Peace is often the least beneficial to those who actually did the fighting for it."

The prince mulled this thought over. He'd never been much of a warrior himself. He knew strategy—he'd studied war—but being a dedicated student and training with a weapons master was much different than employing that weapon in an actual battle. He glanced over at Robin hesitantly. "You don't think it's possible…?"

"What don't I think is possible?"

"Could one of these soldiers…" Oswin's voice dropped even lower. "…be upset enough to attempt to start the war again?"

She eyed him suspiciously. "Start the war again how?"

"Someone had to have let the Nightmare out of The Nothing."

Robin grew silent, and Oswin began to think he might have finally discovered one of the few things which could actually offend the Queen's Rhyme. Her eyes focused on her brother's back as he strode out of the mouth of the cave and into the sunlight. She slowed her pace, dropping a little farther behind. Once she was certain they were out of earshot, she said, "It's not an entirely ridiculous conjecture. But even if some radical did manage to release that creature, I assure you it was completely without the court's knowledge."

"I'm not looking for a direction to point fingers, Robin." Oswin bowed his head and his hair made a curtain around his eyes to diffuse the sudden increase in light as they exited the cave themselves. "But my mother was murdered, my father is dying, and my kingdom lies on the brink of destruction. If I don't find answers soon, we may be too late to fight back."

Robin looked at him, then forward. Her ears twitched and she wiggled her nose a little as she mulled over what he was insinuating. "You want me to ask my brother to spy on his former comrades-in-arms?"

"Not spy," Oswin answered quickly. "Just poke around. See what he can dig up."

"Spy."

"Investigate."

Robin puffed her cheeks out in thought. "He'll never go for it."

Basir, who had apparently been doing some eavesdropping of his own, spoke up. "Someone needs to at least check the door, see if there are any signs of forced entry into

Terra Mirum, speak with the guard or look for clues to who might have opened it for the Nightmare. Ask around the Tulgey Wood. If it leads him to Dream or Fae, so be it. We need to know how this happened, so we know how to combat it."

Robin looked to her husband and nodded. "That," she started, relieved, "I may be able to convince him to agree to." She leapt ahead of the rest of them, the rapid flutter of her wings bringing her in stride with Jack so she could talk to him.

"If he's willing to scout out the area," Oswin explained, "we can use his intelligence and make a proper plan of action at my cousin's."

"Intelligence may be too generous a word for anything related to that man, Your Highness," Basir murmured. "This is the knave who has avoided going back to Arden for years in hopes he can outrun creditors and consequence."

"What kind of consequence?"

Basir shrugged. "Time in prison for...theft, I suppose. He used to be one of Oberon's favored soldiers, and so fancied himself too charming and important to actually pay for...tarts."

Oswin looked bewildered. "He's never returned to Arden because he skipped out on a bill for food?"

"No, Your Highness." Basir gave him an embarrassed smile. "Prostitutes."

Chapter 8

THE TULGEY WOOD

Alys stared dumbly at the hallway entrance. It opened up into an enormous chamber with an impossibly high glass ceiling that allowed the sunlight to pour in as if she were standing outside. The intricate iron frames cast faint, swirling shadows on the floor below.

The trains were large and majestic, not unlike the ones she had seen in pictures or museums, but their glory rather paled in comparison with the impossibly graceful engine she'd seen Oswin board. Still, for all the wonder that the room held, it was rather unsettling. It was bizarrely barren and quiet for a train station. The only noise she heard was what vaguely sounded like the off-kilter ticking of a large clock. No one was boarding the trains. No one was rushing to catch a train. No one even waited patiently for a train to arrive. There was almost no one at all. *Almost*.

Her eyes locked on another group of men in regimental garb. They were talking not a hundred feet from her. She listed to the side, hoping she could go unnoticed, if she stayed close to the wall and snuck behind the large marble pillars that supported the great ceiling above them. She kept her eyes locked on the group, keen on making sure they didn't see her. Their uniforms were identical to the guard who had let her inside the building, but there was something unnervingly different about these men. They were rigid, mechanical, and lifelessly stoic.

She could feel her heart beginning to pound again and hoped to god they couldn't hear it. She peered around the other side of the pillar and noticed more groups on patrol around the perimeter. They kept to the one side of the pillars. A simple back and forth sweep from one side of the room to the other. They stood too stiffly and moved with a precise and technical deftness. So much so that she was almost surprised to see there wasn't a giant winding key sticking out of their backs.

Terrible little toy soldiers.

That was when she realized the echoing through the large chamber was not a clock at all but the marching of feet.

Doom-tek. Doom-tek. Doom-tek.

Alys pressed her back against the pillar, holding her breath, as group of two strode past her. She dropped to her knees and peered again at the group of soldiers still standing in the center of the chamber. As she looked closer, she saw they didn't appear to be talking so much as taking orders from one soldier in particular. He waved one arm up the stairs she'd walked down and five soldiers departed, marching up the stairs, disturbingly in time, to take posts somewhere above.

"You have a lot in common with them, you know," someone remarked quietly.

Alys startled and pivoted towards where she'd been certain there had been merely a large marble pillar just seconds before.

The sunlight fell in such a way that the pillars cast thick vertical shadows on the floor and wall behind them like black piano keys.

Lounging against one such pillar, practically bathing in the absence of sunlight, was a man whose very being seemed to taper off into the air. "You've both lost a train."

"What?" Alys was a little relieved to see it was not a soldier, but she had no reason to trust a possible fellow intruder, either. "I haven't lost a train; I haven't even seen a train. I'm not looking for a train," she lied.

"Well, to be fair, neither are they." He curled long pianist-like fingers and a cigarette materialized between the tips. He brought it to his lips, and this alone seemed to light it. "They're looking for *who's on it*." He exhaled and smoke curled into the air. The smell reminded her more of incense than tobacco.

She looked warily towards the guards, wondering if they could smell it, too.

"But anyone who's seen either of the two would fetch a high price with the Queen, I imagine." He circled around from behind the pillar to linger just beside her, eying the patrolling guards with an odd sense of indifference.

Queen? Alys's nose wrinkled skeptically before his words fully sank in. She slowly rose to a stand so she could keep her voice low. "What sort of price?"

"Your head for theirs." The words were as casual as if he'd merely commented on the weather. He ducked around her again, weaving through the shadows of the other columns.

Alys's form tensed a moment before stumbling after him as quickly and quietly as she could manage. "Wait, w-what? What do you mean, my head?" She whispered, a hand subconsciously resting at her neck.

"I wouldn't worry about it. It doesn't apply to you, remember? *You* haven't seen a train." He led her out of the entryway and away from the trains and troops. Had she been paying attention, she would have seen he'd timed their departure just right so that neither patrol, nor their commander, saw them.

"Well, let's say, for a minute, that it did apply to me."

"Hypothetically?"

"S-sure."

He stopped, turning around so abruptly that Alys tripped backwards against the wall, finding herself face to face with his sternum. He lowered himself until he was more eye level and spoke so quietly that she had to stare at his mouth in order to fully comprehend the words. "We live in desperate times, Dreamer. If you are not with us, you're against us. Do you understand?"

She didn't.

"The Nightmare Queen will stop at nothing until this world is swallowed, and the White Prince is the only thing that stands in the way of that. Anyone with even a passing glance of his whereabouts is at risk if they do not surrender the information." He raised a finger and tapped it lightly between her eyebrows. "And you have more than a passing glance, don't you?"

Alys swallowed hard, her mind spinning with every word he spoke. Wicked Queens and rebel princes—these were the building blocks of fairytales. "This isn't real. Any moment, I'm going to wake up," she concluded through gritted teeth.

"I have no doubt in the power of your mind's creations, Dreamer, but I assure you, this isn't one of them." He looked back towards the train platforms. The commander must have sent another patrol to move down this hall, because the sound of multiple feet hitting the ground at once drew closer.

Doom-tek. Doom-tek. Doom-tek.

"There's something up ahead!" a voice echoed down the hall. They'd been heard, if not seen.

"Move, now!" He pushed himself off the wall, grabbed her wrist with his free hand, and tugged her towards the exit.

High on adrenaline, Alys decided that this stranger was, so far, the lesser of two possible evils and let her feet hit the ground at a run with him.

They made a mad dash into the sunlight, and Alys could hear guards that must have been posted at the door shouting at them. She coughed, their feet kicking up a great deal of dust, but she couldn't figure out where it was coming from as all she could see beneath them was lush grass. As the smell of incense filled her nostrils, she realized it wasn't dust at all but the same smoke from the cigarette he'd lit earlier. And it was beginning to obscure her vision more and more.

She heard them hit what sounded like a metal gate, but her eyes burned if she opened them wide enough to see through the now thick cloud surrounding them. The soft ground beneath her feet now felt like stone, and her shoulders bumped into someone else's — then another and another. The shouts of the guards behind them were drowned out by the sounds of the streets. As the smoke cleared, she realized they'd stumbled into the crowd of a very populated city just outside the abandoned station.

The streets were full enough they disappeared easily into the crowd. His grip on her wrist tightened now that he was in more danger of losing her as they wove through breaks between people.

"If this isn't a nightmare…" Alys coughed the last of the smoke from her lungs. "Why do you keep calling me 'Dreamer'?"

"That's what we've always called your kind." He moved almost without looking, his feet knowing what steps to take to completely throw off anyone attempting to chase after them.

Alys was starting to notice that the people around her were dressed far differently than anything she'd ever seen. "My kind?" She was distracted by the clothing: high collars and top hats, long skirts and coattails. There were vibrant colors and corsets, finely embroidered fabric, feathers and lace.

"Humans capable of passing through our doors, of seeing us when we walk through their world. Most can only conceive us in their sleep through the filter of their subconscious."

Alys tore her gaze away from the clockwork carriage that whirred past them like a wind-up toy, narrowly avoiding being run over. "What?"

"*Pay attention.*" He released her wrist only to grip her elbow so she was forced to match his stride. They ducked into a small alcove, his back to the crowd so that any view of her would be obstructed. "Do not make me repeat myself again." He looked around to make sure no one was paying any attention to either of them before explaining. "In this place, the people around you, including myself, are Dreams, but you are not dreaming." He carefully judged how she accepted this information. "Does that make sense to you?"

"No."

Smoke blew air through his lips and flicked the cigarette towards the building.

It struck the wall and billowed out in small wisps, vanishing into thin air just like it had materialized. "Smoke."

Alys shook her head. "No, thanks.

He grinned. "It's my name."

She looked at him as if to criticize it, but after finding nothing clever to say, she offered her own. "Alyson."

"Alyson," Smoke repeated as if there was something particularly interesting about her giving him that name. He ducked from the alcove and they were on the move again. Smoke led her down a narrow alley. "Not Alys?"

Alys shifted uncomfortably, the name sounding odd coming from this stranger. It left a bitter taste in her mouth. "No," she said quietly. "No one calls me that."

"Charlie did."

Alys's head shot up in shock, which almost immediately melted into white-hot anger when she saw what Smoke held between his fingers—Charlie's note. She quickly checked her pockets, only to find nothing in them. He'd stolen it. She stumbled through her fury, spitting out one cold hard fact that left her sick inside. "Charlie's *dead*."

Smoke's calm and curious expression didn't change, but he did offer the note to her. "I'm sorry."

"Yeah." Alys snatched the note from his hand and shoved it into a back jeans pocket. "You are."

He didn't seem to acknowledge her bitter tone. He was far too busy squinting at her as if trying to look through her or decipher a code from the flecks of gold that intermingled in the honey brown color of her irises.

"What?" Alys snapped after his gaze became far too unnerving to let him continue without explanation.

"Why are you here?"

Alys blinked. It was a very pointed, insistent, kind of question that demanded a very specific answer. "I don't know. It was an accident."

"No."

"No?"

"You may not have intended to come here, Dreamer, but that doesn't mean you weren't meant to."

Alys blinked. "What?"

"We should get going." His refusal to further explain himself was frustrating, but there was a grim and almost paranoid tone in his voice that she was inclined to respect. He took her arm again and pulled her through the alley at a brisk pace, keeping his head down as if making prolonged eye contact with anyone would give them away.

Alys stumbled past stovepipe hats and parasols, her neck craned upward to watch steam rising out of a second chimney on each rooftop, her nose filling with every scent from baking bread to cinders. It was a surreal world, and her ears picked up on the way that every shoe except her own sneakers seemed to make audible clicking noises against the stone streets. A thousand heartbeats tap-danced through their daily activities.

When they reached the city gate, they found it closed, and other than the man in the tower above, it seemed relatively unguarded.

"They must be combing the streets," Smoke murmured. He placed both hands on either side of her shoulders and pushed her back to the wall. "Try to stay quiet."

"What if they see us?"

"What did I *literally* just say?" Smoke's eyes seemed to flash like a cat's in the light. "Bad things, Alys. *Very* bad things if they see us. Now be quiet."

Alys swallowed and nodded.

Smoke's form literally shifted before her eyes, twisting in wisps of the airy substance he took his name from, spiraling downward until it dissipated and left a small housecat in its place.

She stared at the cat.

It looked up at her and flashed a wide, toothy grin.

Alys had never seen a cat grin, and the unnerving sight made her hope she never did again.

The cat moved towards the gate. He went completely unnoticed by the guard, who seemed rather inattentive anyway, and slipped easily through the spaces in the portcullis to the other side. He stopped, turned around, and looked at Alys expectantly.

Again, she stared, and then shook her head, trying her best to mouth, *I can't do that.*

The cat flicked his tail irritably back and forth at her.

Alys sighed and crouched down, slowly moving towards the gate as quietly as possible, her eyes warily glancing up at the tower guard. She tried to keep her mind from lingering on Smoke's words and imagining what 'very bad things' could possibly entail. It was a slow and careful crawl.

The guard noticed nothing and she maneuvered safely to the gate and out of sight.

"I can't get through these," Alys whispered, her hands resting on the portcullis.

"*Shrink*," the cat said as if he were explaining the simplest and most obvious of tasks.

"I can't."

"You won't."

"No," Alys growled. "I *can't*. I can't change my shape like you can."

The cat stared at her incredulously for a moment. He looked past her, ears perking up. "They're coming, Alys."

She looked over her shoulder, panic increasing as she tried to pull up on the metal grate in hopes of lifting it enough that she could sneak under.

"Come on." The cat flattened his ears and flicked his tail back and forth. "Shrink."

Now Alys's ears picked up on the sound of approaching feet all walking in a disturbingly rhythmic synchronization.

"They're coming."

Doom-tek. Doom-tek.

Her heart began to pound in her chest to that same rhythm and she closed her eyes tightly, huddling against the gate and wishing with all her might that she would just wake up. If only it were just a dream. If only she did have the ability to change her size at will. If only she were back on the cold steps, losing horribly at chess.

The cat sighed in frustration and pushed something against her knee with his head.

Alys opened her eyes and saw he had placed a small mushroom on her knee. She looked at him, confused and frightened.

"Eat it, and you will shrink."

There was such a certainty in his voice, and desperation in her veins, that Alys believed him. She scooped the small mushroom up, and, without thinking about it, swallowed it before it had much chance to touch her tongue.

The support of the grate she'd been leaning on seemed to disappear completely from under her, and she found herself falling forward onto the dirt.

Ouch.

Alys felt something soft and furry brush the back of her neck before she was lifted up by the collar of her sweatshirt. She opened her eyes only to find the ground far too many feet away before whatever was carrying her jetted forward.

Alys couldn't help the scream that escaped her as she swung back and forth violently while they rushed onward. She clutched her elbows to her body, desperately trying to ensure that she wasn't going to fall out of her sweatshirt. Normally, she would have tried to comprehend what exactly was going on, but the movement was starting to make her extremely nauseated, and just as she was certain she was going to lose whatever remained of her breakfast from that morning, they stopped. The swinging slowed until, finally, it ceased completely.

Whatever held her swung around, and she realized that not only was she far from the ground, but she was also far away from the city gates. The grass here was insanely overgrown, while the branches of trees loomed overhead. Whatever carried her set her down gently on the ground, and, as her clothing fell back against her neck and shoulders, they felt wet.

"Eww," Alys grumbled, turning around to see the same smoke-colored cat that her companion had shifted into before, but now he was absolutely huge. He towered over her as if she were no larger than a mouse. She even squeaked like one. "How did you do that?"

The cat tilted his head at her with a look that said she was very stupid. It was a far more natural expression for a cat than the grin, but she found she didn't care for it, either.

"Shut up," Alys grumbled.

The cat swished his tail again impatiently and she began to worry he might eat her.

"How do I get back to normal?"

He looked at her long and hard a moment before glancing around. He dashed off briefly into the grass, returning with what looked like some kind of wildflower. It was odd and red and looked nothing like Alys had ever seen before. He dropped it on the ground in front of her. "Take a bite of one of the petals."

"*This* will change me back?"

"If you believe it."

She reached up and tore off a piece of a petal, examining it closely before closing her eyes and taking a bite.

It did not taste good. At all. It tasted like you'd expect a flower petal to taste, the soft texture clinging unfortunately to her tongue as she did her best to swallow it down. When she opened her eyes, the cat was at her feet. While the petal flavor lingered in her mouth, she did appear to be her own size once more.

And then, in another plume of smoke, he was no longer the cat, but the man she'd followed all too blindly through this maddening place. Without so much as another word, he took her arm and tried to lead her down the road again.

"Where are we going?"

"Away from the guards. I thought that much was clear."

Alys pulled her arm away, looking down the path to where it vanished into the woods. "But to where?"

"Now really isn't the time to discuss details," he reminded her, giving a pointed look back at the city.

"No," Alys insisted. "You've bought us some time, and I demand to know where exactly you're taking me."

"Somewhere *safe.*"

Alys huffed skeptically.

Smoke paused in his reply, leaning back to fully take in her folded arms and guarded body language. He looked amused. "You don't trust me."

"Damn right, I don't."

"I haven't given you reason not to trust me," he pointed out.

"You haven't really given me a reason *to* trust you, either."

"Ah." A wide grin spread across his face again. "Are we always this paranoid?"

"I don't know you."

"You know I'm trying to help."

"Do I?"

"I did just save your life." Smoke laughed and shoved his hands in his pockets. "Your caution is admirable, but I'm afraid you're not in much of a position to be questioning the only person who can help you."

"The *only* person?" She pursed her lips, regarding him with a skeptical eye.

"You didn't exactly pick an ideal time to drop in for a visit." He nodded down the path. "Walk with me. At least until we're out of eyesight of the city." He took a few steps and sighed, seeing she hadn't budged. "Of course, if you'd prefer to be seen and questioned by the guards, which will ultimately end in a swift separation of your head from your body—"

"All right, all right!" Alys snapped, jogging a few steps to catch up with him. "So talk."

"You followed someone here."

"I wasn't *following*—"

"That someone is the dethroned prince of Terra Mirum."

"What?" Alys stopped walking, dumbfounded by this new information.

"Terra Mirum. This place. Where you are."

"Os…he's a prince?"

"*Oswin* is a prince, yes. Keep up." He was both chiding her for stumbling over his quick explanation and for lagging behind. "His mother, our late Queen, was murdered—"

"Murdered?"

Smoke glared at her. "We're on a bit of

a tight schedule, so I'd appreciate it if you'd stop interrupting—"

"S-sorry." A second after she did it, Alys hated herself a little for apologizing.

"Thank you. *Murdered*." He said the word very deliberately as if he were returning to reading something aloud. "She was murdered by a Nightmare that escaped from The Nothing." He put his finger up as if expecting her to interrupt again.

He would have been right.

"In the same right that we are Dreams, there are Nightmares, and Nightmares spawn in The Nothing where they, under normal circumstances, live out their existence only managing to terrorize anyone through the subconscious—get it?"

"Um…"

"Good." His pace seemed to quicken and she began to wonder what exactly they seemed to be running late for. "Oswin escaped to your world where, for a day's time, he was able to elude the Nightmare and any of her puppets completely. Unfortunately…" He came to a natural but abrupt stop, like a cat when it thinks its prey may have seen it.

He continued the conversation, but there was something breathless and unsupported about his voice—a sudden hush and loss of vocal focus. "He then ran into you, thus bringing you here, and that does...complicate things."

Alys could feel a pit forming in her stomach. "How?"

He didn't answer, but rather seemed distracted by something he'd seen beyond the trees.

"Is there something you're not telling me?"

"Oh, countless things." Smoke smiled. "But that really isn't important right now." He finally turned to face her. "What's important right now is the Tulgey Wood."

"The what?"

"It's a particular part of the Forest of Thought," he elaborated, vaguely waving at the forest in front of them. "The Forest of Thought being the largest and thickest crop of trees in all of Terra Mirum." It was unremarkable looking, really, and the only way Alys could think to describe it would be that it was the kind of place you didn't want to walk through after dark, but, then again, she felt most forests fell in that category.

"O…kay?"

"You're going to walk down this path—"

"Why?" Alys interrupted.

Smoke exhaled through his nostrils. "Do you want to get home?"

Alys averted her eyes slightly, not entirely sure where home was, let alone if she had any desire to return to it.

"Forgive me. Let me pose a simpler question, would you like to avoid *execution*?" Smoke did nothing to hide his growing irritation with the girl. "…yes."

"Good," he said tersely. "Then you are going to walk down this path until you come to a strange old building with a lot of books."

"Like a library?" Alys asked.

Smoke hesitated but a moment. "Yes. A library. Of Sorts. There you will speak to a man by the name of Mr. Smith. Do you understand?" He lowered his voice, but this time there was an unnerving sense of urgency to it.

"You're not coming with me?" Again she felt suspicious.

"No." He offered no explanation as to why, but she had the feeling it had something to do with whatever had distracted him before by the way his eyes shifted in that direction once more. "But I will meet you there later. Mr. Smith will ask you a series of questions, and it is imperative that you answer every single one, regardless of how ridiculous they may seem. Do you understand?"

"I guess?"

"Keep your mind on Mr. Smith and that library. Do not let it wander, and whatever you do, *do not* step off the path."

Her throat felt dry. "Why not?"

"Trust me, my dear. You wouldn't want to get lost."

Chapter 9

LOST IN THOUGHT

"I'm not sure this is the right way," Oswin murmured, looking around the forest, unable to recognize even so much as a leaf in it.

"Because it's not," Robin said flatly.

"It's the right way," Jack answered, biting back his irritation poorly.

"No, I really think we came out on the wrong side of the Tulgey Wood," Oswin answered. He wasn't *trying* to begin another confrontation with the Fae, yet he couldn't help but feel they were lost.

"Trust me, Your Highness. I know Thought like the back of my hand, and this is the way to the Duchess' manor," Jack answered through gritted teeth. He took a deep breath. "Once I have you on track, I'll investigate the door and meet you there."

"Actually…" Someone took a loud bite out of something crunchy. "…Oswin is right." Smoke was lounging in a tree devoid of any apples. Though he'd only just arrived, his posture, and the way he casually snacked on one of the apples, suggested he'd been waiting there for hours.

Basir started a little by his sudden appearance and Robin put a hand on her husband's arm to keep him from falling over. "How did you…?"

Jack scowled, knowing that Smoke's presence meant he was no longer even remotely in charge.

"Have you been following us?" Oswin asked incredulously.

"No, I've been tracking the girl like I said I would," Smoke answered. "I just ran into you lot by pure happenstance."

"What girl?" Jack asked.

Basir's eyes widened. "So she *is* in Terra Mirum."

Smoke pointed to Basir and then his own nose, then to Basir again as he hopped down. "She's close, too." He tossed the half-eaten apple over his shoulder. It bounced once off the ground and dissipated into a wisp of vapor.

"What girl?" Jack repeated, but the question still went unanswered.

"You know the Duchess lives on the other side of the Tulgey Wood, right?" Smoke asked.

Jack's face flushed. He wasn't entirely sure if it was out of embarrassment or anger.

"Ah. Then how would we get to the Nothing from here?" Robin asked, more for validation than information.

"I know how to get to The Nothing," Jack said, his jaw tightening and hands balling into fists at his sides.

"Why do you want to get to The Nothing?" Smoke looked at them .

"Someone needs to look into it," Oswin explained. "See if we can find out who let the Nightmare out, or maybe a clue as to who got us into this mess. Nightmares don't typically just decide to go for a stroll in Terra Mirum. It may help us figure out how to combat this thing, see what we're truly up against."

Smoke looked pleasantly surprised at Oswin's good idea, and Oswin tried not to look insulted by Smoke's level of surprise. "Smart plan," he congratulated the man. "Perhaps you'll make a half-decent King, after all." He looked back at Jack a moment. "Except you're sending *Jack* to investigate? By himself?"

Jack snorted angrily. "What are you saying?"

"I'm not saying, I'm insinuating." Smoke grinned at him. "And what I'm insinuating is that two heads are better than one, of course."

"Are you volunteering to go with him?" Basir raised a dark eyebrow.

"I can do it on my own," Jack said. He felt his responsibility and authority slipping through his fingers, and he was desperately trying not to sound like a petulant child in the process. "You don't have to worry."

"That might be good idea, actually," Robin advised. "The Nightmare's influence stretches further and further out from the castle. There is a certain safety in numbers."

Jack sighed and nodded, conceding to the point. "*Fine.*" He rested his wrist on the hilt of his sword. "If you're so worried about safety, we'll go together."

"And it'll keep you out of any brothels you happen to pass," she added casually.

"That was *one* time, Robin. *One* time."

"It was one time you got *caught.*"

"What about the *girl?*" Basir's question drew everyone's attention. "We can't just let her wander around with a Nightmare on the loose."

"She *wandered* this way," Smoke said levelly. "We may even find her as we go. I promise you, I will find her."

"If you do…" Robin hesitated, uncomfortable with her own warning. "Be careful not to encourage any…*thoughts.*"

"You of all people should know that no one can control the thoughts of a young woman." Smoke was charming and playful, and it was completely unwelcomed to Robin in that moment.

"You know what I'm talking about."

"I don't," Jack said indignantly, his patience gone, but his presence still thoroughly ignored.

"I do and I won't." At least he wouldn't *anymore*…probably. Smoke turned to Oswin standing on his heel. "You know how to get to the Duchess' on your own from here?"

The Prince looked back in the general direction they'd come from. "I think so."

"Then safe travel to the lot of you." Smoke turned to Jack, and the two men started off in the opposite direction. "We'll rendezvous at the manor."

Robin lingered as she watched them go, unable to ignore the sinking feeling growing in the pit of her stomach. "Keep on the windy side of care," she whispered after them.

Oswin placed a reassuring hand on her shoulder. "Let's go."

***

Unbeknownst to Alys or Oswin, they were but a short distance from each other. In fact, had Smoke not directed his party's attention towards him, and had Alys not been so focused on the path, they might have even caught a glimpse of one another.

Thought, even more so than the rest of the world around it, was a peculiar place. It was both mercurial and invariably malleable. So, by thinking of nothing but the path and the library, she could truly see nothing but the path and the library. Her mind began to wander a little, drifting away from Mr. Smith to what kind of library he might be in charge of. Was it very big? Did it have many books? Were they fiction or reference? Would she maybe be able to take a book with her? What kind of importance did such a great library have?

And then a book nearly fell on her head.

Alys sidestepped the hardback volume that fell from the trees with a frantic flutter and a loud thud. She looked upward, expecting to see someone sitting on a branch who had accidentally dropped their book, but there was nothing there so mundane. Instead, she saw a great tree whose leaves appeared to be made of pages, and, instead of bearing fruit or flowers, sprouted novels. Some were still very small and young, while some were overripe and rotting, with pages bursting from the binding.

She looked back at the book that had nearly knocked her unconscious. Its cover was black and sleek, emblazoned with gold lettering, and displayed a heart covered in clockwork gears. "*Steel & Sky, Tales of the Dead Man* by Ren Cummins," Alys read aloud. She had an odd sense that the book smiled at her, but immediately dismissed it because, of course, books didn't smile.

She knelt down by it and carefully pulled back the cover to peek inside. It seemed like an ordinary book—it didn't talk or start to glow. Yet there was something about the way it laid open that seemed akin to a child holding its arms out, just dying to be held.

Not twenty feet away, another dull thud hit the ground and she looked up, startled. A second book had fallen from another tree.

It was then that she noticed that the book tree was not unique to this forest and she had wandered into a literal orchard of books. She spied a book on one of the reachable branches—it was very plain looking and makeshift. It simply read *Lock & Steele* in scrawled handwriting like the title wasn't permanent. She reached out to pluck it from the tree.

"Oh, please don't do that," a kind voice said, and she turned to see a woman balancing a basket of books against her hip. She reminded Alys of the librarian at her school, only far better dressed. Simple yet classy, she wore tweed slacks and a brown vest that had been tailored to her. Her blouse was rolled up at the sleeves, but the high collar stood up around her throat and the white fabric accentuated the warm chestnut color of her skin. The very picture of the sophisticated bookworm. Her hair, Alys noticed, consisted of small braids that were swept back into a tight bun at the base of her neck. Spectacles sat on the bridge of her nose, which complemented the smile crossing her lips.

Alys shrank away like a child caught with her hand in a cookie jar.

"It's not ready yet," the Librarian explained as she bent down to pick up Mr. Cummins' book and placed it in the basket with the rest. "Still being written."

Alys looked back at the book she'd attempted to pick and noticed that it was both adding and losing pages. "Oh…"

"I have plenty others, if you're interested."

Alys shook her head. "No, I don't think I have time."

"There's always time for a good story."

Alys smiled. "I really shouldn't."

"Pity," the Librarian commented and started walking toward the next tree. "I have just the book for you."

"Is there a library nearby?" Alys followed her.

"Of course." The Librarian smiled warmly. "Where do you think I keep all of these?"

"I couldn't even begin to imagine."

"Would you like to see it?"

Alys smiled, her heart skipping a beat. "Very much."

The Librarian led her through the orchard, a few books falling from the trees behind them as they walked.

Alys pointed to some of the rotting volumes. "What are those?"

"Oh. Sad, isn't it?" The Librarian *tsked* and shook her head. "Those are the lost causes--tales that will never be finished, continuously overworked until they rot and are useless to everyone, even the author."

"Does it happen a lot?"

"Only when vanity, pride or obsession overpowers the wit of that being written."

"So...?"

"Constantly."

The maze of trees thinned out into a small clearing that seemed to exist only to showcase the building before them. It was an organic-looking structure. Trees sprouted from the ground and wove upwards, the branches tangling with each other to create a living fretwork roof. They passed through heavy, leather-bound doors, and the pleasant smell of aging paper greeted them.

"Welcome to the Phrontistery. Home of every story ever written, and quite a few that will never be."

The library itself was breathtaking. Alys had never seen so many books in one location, and it absolutely elated her. She craned her neck upwards, unable to stop the grin from spreading across her face. "Oh...my... god." She moved along the shelves, running her fingers over the spines, taking in every title. "I've never seen anything more beautiful in my entire life."

The Librarian smiled warmly, setting the basket of books on a desk. "Some are only thoughts or concepts. Some are epic tales, and others just short stories. All vastly valuable." She began to peruse the titles. "Ah, here we are." She pulled an impossibly large book from the shelf and moved to Alys' side. "I believe this is what you need."

Alys reluctantly tore her gaze away from the endless row of volumes she'd been studying moments before. She tilted her head to the side, reading the title embossed in gold on the spine of the tome cradled in the other woman's arms. It had an encyclopedia-like quality about it, and she realized that similar books lined the entire bottom row of the shelves as far as the eye could see. "*The History of Ever?*"

The Librarian nodded. "Volume II." She held it out towards Alys. "Well, go on, take it. It's not the lightest thing, you know."

Alys tentatively took it, straining against the weight as the Librarian transferred it completely into her care. "What am I supposed to do with this?"

The Librarian shook her head with a small smile. "Read it, of course." She gestured to an empty bookstand at the end of the aisle.

"The whole thing?" Alys asked incredulously, awkwardly hefting the book up with a great sigh. She gulped, trying to imagine how long this volume was alone, let alone the entire collection. "How many of these even are there?"

"No, just the relevant parts of that particular volume," came the Librarian's cryptic answer. "This series is still being written. *Ever* is still going on, you might have noticed."

Alys nodded awkwardly, then looked back at the book. She wasn't even sure what Volume II of the *History of Ever* even contained, let alone what parts would be relevant. Nothing about it looked particularly intriguing. Or useful. "I'm sorry, why do I need this?" She looked up, but the Librarian had already picked up the basket again to find a home for the recently harvested stories. She sighed and turned back to the book, peering at it skeptically. She cautiously opened it, and the spine cracked, kicking up a full breath of dust as old as history itself.

The aged pages were covered with black and white photos, sketches, and the tiniest print text she'd ever seen. Even with perfect vision she found herself squinting. She reached for a magnifying glass hanging from the stand, and when she focused on the words, she found they weren't English.

F'iel brillig, en va slithy toves
Mor gyre en gimble eck va wabe:
Ra mimsy halam va borogoves
En va mome raths outgrabe.

She blinked and shook her head. It wasn't simply that she didn't understand the words, but her eyes were having trouble focusing on the words themselves. As she strained to see the font clearly, the words shifted into focus, some even changing shape to words she recognized. Others did not translate, but their context helped her figure out their meaning.

"Beware the Jabberwock, my son!
The jaws that bite, the claws that catch!
Beware the Jubjub bird, and shun
The frumious Bandersnatch!"

He took his vorpal sword in hand;
Long time the manxome foe he sought—
So rested he by the Tumtum tree
And stood awhile in thought.

And, as in uffish thought he stood,
The Jabberwock, with eyes of flame,
Came whiffling through the Tulgey Wood,
And burbled as it came!

One, two! One, two! And through and through
The vorpal blade went snicker-snack!
He left it dead, and with its head
He went galumphing back."

Alys's face clouded over in confusion. She looked at a sketch of some kind of dragon straight from the fantasy stories she'd buried herself in when she wasn't working or spending time with Charlie. Its body was great in size and covered in razor-like scales from the terrifying horns on its head to the alarmingly sharp-looking spikes on its tail. Thick, leathery wings were extended with a wingspan that was easily twice its body length, and even though it was nothing more than a drawing, the eyes seemed to possess an unearthly glow. The terrifying illustration bore a single caption: *Jabberwock.*

Below the drawing, in somehow even tinier print, she read aloud the definition, "'Jabberwocks mutate from Dreams that have been overexposed to The Nothing, or a similar energy. Due to its mercurial nature, it can take many forms and exists as one of the most dangerous breeds of Nightmares (*See Horrors).'"

Alys blinked and let her grip on the magnifying glass slacken. She stood up straight with a confused, albeit informed, "Huh…?"

"So," the Librarian said as she returned, beaming with a knowing grin as she sidled up beside Alys. "I trust you found what you needed?"

"Uh…no." Alys admitted. "Not even slightly."

The Librarian's face fell, bewildered, as if she'd never encountered such a situation like this before.

"But, to be fair, I'm not looking for a book," Alys said quickly. "I'm looking for Mr. Smith."

"Mr. Smith?"

"Yeah," Alys said. "Is he here?"

The Librarian shook her head. "No, of course not. This is a place where nothing is ever forgotten, even the things that have never happened."

"Oh. Okay?" Alys paused. "Am I in the wrong place? Like, is there more than one library in this forest?"

"Ah." The Librarian looked Alys up and down with a warm smile. "Are you lost?"

She smiled helplessly. "More than you can possibly imagine."

"That's wonderful," the Librarian said, seemingly struck with awe and admiration.

"Wonderful?"

"Of course," the Librarian answered eagerly. "It's the best place for anyone to be."

Alys took a deep breath and a laugh of disbelief escaped her. "No, I'm sorry. I don't think you understand."

"But I do understand." The other woman took her hand. "Think of all the things you're bound to see."

"What?" Alys wriggled her hand free. She was starting to suspect that the complete indifference to personal space was a widely held custom in this world.

The Librarian sighed and shook her head. "When you know where you're going, you're almost certain to get there sooner or later. However, when you're lost, you never know what you'll find! It could be quite an adventure."

"But I don't want an adventure. I want to find Mr. Smith!"

"No, I don't believe you actually do," the

Librarian continued in the same irritatingly level tone. "If you did, you would be there."

"I would be there if I knew the way," Alys explained, losing her patience. "But I don't know the way. So I need you to *tell me* the way so I can get where I want to go."

"You don't need anything from me, my dear. If you truly wanted to be there, you'd know the way."

"That doesn't make any sense!" Alys snapped.

"It makes all the sense in the world. You're just not listening." The Librarian clasped her hands in front of her with a deep exhalation.

Alys pinched the bridge of her nose and, while making a great effort to suppress a scream, a stifled squeak escaped her instead. "Look, can you please just tell me how to get to Mr. Smith?"

"If I told you how to find your way, it wouldn't be yours."

Alys stared at the Librarian. She cleared her throat, trying to keep the acid from her tone and her frustration in check. "I beg your *pardon*?"

"I said if I told you how to find your way—"

"*No*, I know what you said. I was just hoping you would change your answer." She took a deep breath. "I'm sorry I lost my temper. I'm just really frustrated and confused right now, not to mention incredibly lost. I don't know where I am or how to get where I was told to go, so if you could please tell me how to find the way, I would be extremely grateful."

The Librarian adjusted her spectacles, and the look she fixated on the Dreamer could only be described as one of pity. "I'm sorry, Alys. That's a road you have to find on your own."

The library filled with the sound of Alys's frustrated growl as she stormed out.

***

"So," Jack said now that he and Smoke were alone. "...what girl?"

"You're predictable," Smoke sad, his attention far more focused on their surroundings. "Keep an eye out. We don't know if the Nightmare was the only thing to get out. It would have been very easy for a Tove or two to slip out."

"I'm just trying to have a friendly conversation," Jack said, gesturing around them. "Brighten up the gloomy surroundings. Make the trip a little more enjoyable."

"She's not your type," said Smoke flatly.

"How do you know my type?"

"Well, for starters, to impress her, you'd have to rely on your charm rather than your coin purse."

"You and Robin are never going to let that go, are you?" Jack sighed.

"The fact that you exiled yourself from Arden due to a mounting debt at Love in Idleness? No. No, I don't imagine we'll be letting that go any time soon," Smoke chuckled.

"She better than your Duchess? This mystery girl?"

Smoke glanced sideways at the other man. "No." His demeanor bristled.

Jack grinned, and seeing he'd struck a nerve, he chose to dance on it further. "It's just you're keeping the whole thing pretty secret. It makes me wonder if you're trying to hide something more than a simple mission—"

"She's a Dreamer."

Jack grew suddenly quiet. "You're not serious."

Smoke looked back at him, no mirth in his eyes.

"*Now*? Of all times? How did she even get in?"

"She followed the prince here, so, as you can imagine, it's important that I find her soon before anyone, or *anything* else, does."

"Then why are you here with me?"

"Because I may have forgotten to mention that I know where she's going," Smoke answered.

"So you lied to Robin and that lot."

"I neglected to mention a detail that didn't seem particularly important at the time."

Jack grinned widely. "You lied to *royalty*."

"It was hardly the first time." Smoke shrugged. "Besides, there's no harm in it. She'll still be there by the time we're done."

"You still didn't have to come with me."

"I didn't," Smoke admitted. "I wanted to. Frankly, I'm just as curious about who opened the door as you are."

"You're not just supervising me?" Jack almost smiled. "Sir, I'm almost touched. You finally trust me to get a job done right on my own."

"Shut up."

"I'm only partially yanking your chain here. Truly, that means a lot to me."

"No." Smoke dropped his voice to a hurried whisper. "I mean be quiet. I hear something."

Jack grew suddenly still and the two listened intently.

It was muffled by the trees around them and the soft ground beneath their feet, but the sound was undeniable.

Doom-tek.

The heartbeat-like march of feet stomping together. A patrol — and it was close.

"What are they doing back here?" Smoke asked. "Do they intend to open the door again?"

"We have to move," Jack said quietly. "They'll be on us soon."

A gunshot rang out, and air rushed between them, making their hair stand on end.

"Halt, in the name of the Queen!"

The two left the path and took off into the trees, leaping over roots and under branches.

The sound of tree branches crashing down behind them added to the percussion of gunshots, but even during the cacophony that pierced their ears, the rhythm of the soldiers' march was discernible. It was gaining speed, but every foot remained in time with every other.

"We should split up," Jack called to his companion, hoping his words would be drowned out by their pursuers' own gunshots. "Regroup once we've lost them."

Smoke glanced behind them reluctantly. "At the door?"

"Agreed!"

Smoke's form exhaled into the incense-like mist, which blew upwards and away as if caught by the wind. In a mere blink, he was gone.

Jack turned abruptly to the right, able to move much quicker unhindered by a companion as he bounced from tree to tree, his feet never fully touching the ground.

Alys emerged from the orchard, fuming, careful to sidestep any falling books. Why did everyone in this place speak in nothing but riddles? Why were they all so dramatic and cryptic? And why…?

Alys paused a moment, realizing she'd never actually told the Librarian her name, and yet…

Despite returning to exactly where she believed she had been prior to entering the Phrontistery, the path itself was nowhere to be seen. Her brow furrowed and she walked a little farther out, looking for any discoloration in the forest floor that would indicate the beaten path she'd been walking on not half an hour prior.

She laughed nervously. Suddenly she became keenly aware of every warning Smoke had given her when she entered the Tulgey Wood. She took a deep breath as she attempted to retrace her steps—or what she thought was retracing her steps, anyway, but the more she wandered, the less familiar anything looked.

"Okay, Alys," she began to reason out loud. "Don't panic. The light's just changed a little since you were last out here, that's all. It has to be here, okay? It has to. Paths don't just vanish on their own. That's impossible."

"On the contrary," a man in a dark gray suit addressed her. "Anything is possible."

"Quite possible," said another man beside him in a slightly lighter gray suit. "It's really just a matter of bending the rules."

"Rules are very bendable, you see," the first man explained.

"Rather like rubber," the second agreed.

"One just has to have the mind to bend it."

Alys wasn't sure what to make of either man or either shade of gray. It was hard to tell them apart as the only differences between them were the slight variation in the color of their suits and that one wore a bowler hat while the other a fedora. If she listened carefully, the man in the bowler appeared to have an accent befitting an Englishman while the fedora-topped fellow sounded like a very well-spoken American. The accents were hardly worth noting, the differences beginning to blur, and Alys began to forget them almost as soon as she'd noted them.

"Okay, but a path doesn't have a mind—it's a path," Alys reasoned.

"Well," the second man scoffed. "Perhaps it was you who had the mind to move away from it."

"Okay, maybe I did—" Alys half confessed before the first interrupted.

"A-ha!"

"But I didn't move far!" she quickly countered.

"In Thought, even baby steps are a giant leap," the second informed her.

"It was just for a few minutes!"

"Even still, did you really expect it to sit around and wait for you?" the first man asked. "It's a path. It has places to be."

"Yes, I know, but—" Alys stopped short, staring at both men for a moment of confused silence. "I'm sorry. What did you just say?"

"It has places to be," he repeated. "Paths get around. They know most places worth knowing. They're very hurried things. They must be followed or they'll just go on without you."

"That's not…" Alys breathed, unable to finish.

"Possible?" the first man smiled knowingly.

"But we've just told you." The second man spoke patiently. "Anything is possible."

The first gave a stiff nod. "Never say never."

"Why not?"

The two paused, dumbfounded by what, to them, seemed to be a very silly question.

"Because…" The second man struggled for a moment. "Reasons."

"It's too limiting," the first interjected.

"Yes!" the second squeaked. "You're not

allowing yourself to see the spectrum."

"I…" Alys gave a tight smile. "I think you've lost me."

"There's no such thing as black and white," they both answered in disturbingly perfect unison.

"We should know," the first man chuckled.

"We're the experts on it," the second bragged.

"I'm Mr. Earnest Grey." The first removed his bowler.

"And I'm Mr. Frank Gray." The second tipped his fedora.

"Ah…" Alys was beginning to worry she'd stumbled on two mentally unstable people. "So you're brothers, then?"

Mr. Grey and Mr. Gray looked at each other for a moment before denying this assumption with a suspiciously choreographed shake of their heads.

"Oh," Alys answered. "So it's only a coincidence that you have the same name?"

"They *aren't* the same," Mr. Grey said indignantly.

"They aren't?" Alys echoed, wondering if perhaps she'd heard them incorrectly.

"No," Mr. Gray reasoned. "I am a Mr. *Gray* and he is a Mr. *Grey*. Do you hear the difference?"

"It's very subtle," Mr. Grey said after seeing Alys's hopeless expression.

"Oh." Alys nodded, forcing another tight smile. "Yeah, I totally hear it now," she lied.

They produced business cards and Mr. Grey said, "Grey and Gray, experts on the various shades of grey."

"And gray," Mr. Gray added.

"The various shades of gray?" Alys wondered aloud.

"And grey," Mr. Grey added importantly.

"What does that mean, exactly?"

"It means," Mr. Gray went on just as importantly. "That nothing is definite. There is no right or wrong. There is no up or down, nor right or left. It's our task to navigate the spectrum in Thought."

"The world is infinite," Mr. Grey continued. "So there really are no sides—just the in-between. Does that make sense?"

"Kinda?"

"Then, *frankly*, there is no such thing as white," Mr. Gray concluded.

"And, in all *earnestness*, there is no such thing as black," Mr. Grey responded with glee.

"Only shades of grey?" Alys was starting to feel dizzy.

"Yes," said Mr. Grey, who was very excited at being able to explain this to her. Alys got the feeling they didn't often encounter many other people. "And if I may be frank—"

"But I'm Frank," protested Mr. Gray.

Mr. Grey looked put out. "I could be a marvelous Frank."

"That doesn't matter," Mr. Gray said, and crossed his arms much like a petulant child would upon being denied ice cream. "I'm Frank, end of story."

"Well, yes, of course you are," Mr. Grey said patiently. "But, look, I could do a lovely impersonation…"

At this point, Alys had stopped listening. They were engaged enough in their own squabble that they'd forgotten she was even there. It was a bizarrely familiar feeling, being alone when in the company of others. It reminded her of Appleweed. The way you could have a million eyes on you and still not be seen. It made her heart ache, and, for the first time since she was a child, Alys remembered what it felt like to be truly lonely.

And then she saw him.

Staring back at her, hidden ever so slightly behind a tree. She recognized the red hoodie first, then the blonde curls that fell loosely around his face.

"Charlie?"

Chapter 10

THE OFFICE OF OBLIVION

Alys stared in disbelief, and while the argument around her did not cease, her senses focused so intensely on the sight in front of her that all other things seemed to fade from existence. Color drained from everything but him, and the world was muffled into silence as she side-stepped the two arguing men and moved towards what she could only assume was a ghost. "Charlie?"

Charlie didn't answer, but once she'd crept close enough that she knew her eyes could not be deceiving her, he turned away, moving farther into the forest.

"Wait!"

She picked up her pace, and so did he, and though she kept her eyes locked on the red of his sweatshirt, somewhere in the back of her mind she began to notice her surroundings changing. The closer she moved towards him, the thicker the trees seemed to get, and less and less sunlight broke through the branches. She stumbled over roots and he gained more distance. "Charlie! Stop!"

The trees had made a narrow kind of hallway that she ran down. She could see the silhouette of her friend now. It was strange. She was running as fast as she could, but even though Charlie was clearly walking, she could not catch up to him.

Charlie made his way to a clearing in the trees. The ground was harder, frozen solid beneath their feet. The temperature had dropped, and the trees surrounding the area seemed to crane away from the center, the trunks somehow hardened and petrified, dusted with frost.

At the center of the circular clearing was a singular tree, far different from any other in the forest. Its bark was smooth and obsidian—like any color or texture had been burned from it some time ago. The shape of the tree was gnarled, and while completely barren of leaves, countless branches reached out in every direction. At some point, it had been clearly split in two, but the tall branches had tangled with each other on top, as if some life still persisted in it. Curiously, someone had set a large crooked door to fill the gap between the two halves, as if bracing them to stay apart. Even curiouser, as far as Alys could tell, was that the door itself didn't appear to go anywhere.

No birds chirped. No frogs croaked. Even the air was dead here.

It was as if he had been waiting for her. He stood there just long enough for her to begin to clear the thicket before approaching the door.

"Charlie!" Alys called again, stumbling a little as she climbed over a particularly large root.

He hesitated, turning to look at her. His face had never been so hauntingly familiar. Every aspect of him was simultaneously sur-real and painfully present in that moment. He smiled at her, the sad, reluctant smile that had meant to encourage her so many times before when they parted ways. It was the smile she used to say goodbye to. The "I'll miss you" smile. The "I hope to see you tomorrow" smile. The smile she couldn't recall seeing the last time they'd said their goodbyes. Then he opened the door and seamlessly slipped inside.

Alys inhaled sharply and rushed ahead, flinging the door open without a thought.

The silence broke.

Shrieks that could belong to none other than the damned themselves escaped through the door by way of a biting wind that rushed around her. She squinted through the dark that seemed to be leaking out like the smoke from a backdraft. The icy air sliced and bit at her hands and face, attempting to both lacerate and pull her in with each gust. What she saw in that dizzying moment was not Charlie or anything at all. She gazed into an endless space: vacuous, dark, and hungry.

"Charlie!" She cried over the howling noises, her eyes watering with each whip of cold wind.

Through that absolute nothing, blue eyes met hers, and she saw flashes of blonde hair just before the door slammed shut.

Alys blinked hard before her eyes focused on a hand pressed against the door. Her gaze tracked up the arm until she found herself staring at a now familiar face.

"You're really terrible at following directions. You know that, don't you?" Smoke mused.

Alys looked from him to the door again, shaken. "W-what was that?"

"Nothing."

"That was *not* nothing," Alys protested, reaching a shaking hand up to wipe at her eyes.

"No, not nothing as in something to be ignored." Smoke answered. "*The* Nothing. The literal manifestation of the absence of life and everything. Why did you go off the path?"

"B-but it, it was—"

"A vast and indescribable emptiness. The loss of every happy notion in your mind. An all-consuming darkness that would eat up the world, given a chance. Yes, all of these. Path. You went off it. Why?"

Alys tried to push his hand off the door. "I saw Charlie go in there. That thing has him, and we have to help—"

"No, Alys." Smoke's voice had softened to a tone she wasn't particularly comfortable with him using on her. It was too familiar and too kind to be used by anyone who knew her so little. He took a deep breath. "You didn't see Charlie. You couldn't have seen Charlie."

"I *did*. I know it sounds crazy, but it was him! Just like the day I last saw him. He was even wearing his red sweatshirt."

"Exactly as you remember him," Smoke said quietly. "Down to the way you looked at each other."

"Yes! He…" Alys's voice slowly trailed off as she began to understand the look in the man's eyes. A melancholic silence fell between them, and Alys looked back to the iron handle she still had in her hand. She slowly released it. "This place…it can lie, can't it?"

"The Tulgey Wood is not safe for you alone — or anyone like you. It will show you exactly what you want to see, or, in some cases, exactly what you don't want to see in order to keep you here. I'm sorry, Alys, but wherever Charlie is, it isn't in Terra Mirum."

Alys sunk back on her heels and looked from him to the door. "Okay," she said weakly. "Why did it bring me here, then?" She gestured to the door.

"Are you particularly susceptible to nightmares?"

There was an obvious hesitation. "No," Alys lied.

Smoke met her eyes with an expression that didn't believe her. "Well, then, I have no idea. Probably just a coincidence."

There was a moment where both lies hung in the air between them, neither believing the other had been fooled, but both parties refusing to actually call attention to it. And since Smoke had not directly called her bluff, and Alys had not caved and confessed, they moved on as if either lie had never happened.

Smoke looked around for a moment. "Was there no one here when you arrived?"

Alys shook her head. "Should there have been?"

"At least two guards, if memory serves." He dropped to his knees, but found no evidence of a scuffle or violence. He gently pushed her back so he could examine the side of the door. Nothing out of the ordinary. "Someone...opened it."

"Yeah, me, just now," Alys pointed out.

"No, before that." Smoke dismissed her statement as he walked the circumference of the tree, finding absolutely nothing at all out of the ordinary. "The Nightmare I told you about? This is where she came from. But there's no sign of struggle, no damage to the door, nothing, which means someone had to have opened it from this side."

"I'm not sure I follow."

"It means someone actually let that monster out on purpose," Smoke said grimly.

"That sounds bad," Alys said.

"It *is* bad." The man took a deep breath and just stood there a moment, assessing the situation before placing his hand on her shoulder. He turned her around and walked her back through the thicket. "This way."

"Where are we going?" Alys asked, noticing that once they passed the first ring of petrified trees, somehow the rest of the forest became more spread out and less threatening than it had been on her journey towards the clearing.

"I'm taking you somewhere safe," Smoke answered, and they stopped a mere twenty feet from the clearing, where they found the same path that Alys had lost some hours ago.

"I don't understand. This literally wasn't here a minute ago," Alys protested.

"I'm sure it wasn't," Smoke agreed, giving her a patronizing pat on the shoulder before falling into stride beside her. "Now, we're going to Mr. Smith's, okay? Keep your mind on him and his...library."

"I did. I kept my mind completely on his library. I still got lost."

"But not Mr. Smith himself?" Smoke asked.

"I've never met him. How can I keep my mind on him?"

"With that kind of attitude, it's no wonder you got lost."

Alys sighed and looked down, keeping her eyes on the path as if she suspected it might attempt to move out from under her at any moment. "Where did you go?"

"Look up," Smoke answered facetiously.

"I mean *before*," Alys grumbled.

"I had...an *errand* to run."

"An errand?"

"Checking in on things. You know—an errand."

"Okay." Alys wasn't buying it, but, just as before, she decided to not draw attention to it directly. It had become a custom to their conversations. One blatantly lying, the other pretending to believe them. "Then how did you know where I was?"

"I didn't. I just happened to be in the area."

"Uh-huh." There was an entire world of skepticism in just that one acknowledgement. "Things often 'just happen' with you?"

"I'm a terribly lucky fellow," Smoke explained. "Watch your head."

Alys looked up at him. "Watch my—ouch!" She stumbled backward, rubbing her temple, which had knocked hard into a solid wood door. She blinked and looked at it. It was sturdy enough, but firmly attached to a rather dilapidated looking frame that somehow remained standing even after Alys' collision.

"Peculiar amount of doors lying about in this forest," Smoke chimed unhelpfully. "They'll sneak up on you if you aren't careful."

Alys tried to glare at him, but it made her head ache, and so she looked back towards the door in front of them. It had an old look about it. The wood stain on the oak looked nearly antique, and ivy had wrapped around it in such a way that she wondered if it was even still possible to open it. Unlike the previous door, this one was inset in a large grey stone building, cracked and dimpled by time. Spider webs hung from nearly every possible place, but for some reason, appeared abandoned by their tenants. The flora which had grown up and over the roof, hiding most of the building from view, looked half-starved and gnarled, despite the rather healthy plants and trees that stood not ten feet from them. It was an unwanted building, a place that even the wildlife had chosen not to remember.

"This is a library? This place looks abandoned."

Smoke nodded. "It usually is."

She reached up and moved aside some of the ivy to reveal a tarnished brass plate that had been engraved with one word: *Oblivion.*

Alys felt the hair on the back of her neck stand on end, and she looked back at Smoke warily. "What is this place?"

"Mr. Smith's office," he said.

Alys held his gaze and persisted, her

voice a little firmer now. "Yes, but why are we here?"

"He needs you to answer a few questions."

"You said." Alys spoke through gritted teeth, growing impatient with cryptic answers to direct questions. "But *why*?"

"If I told you, you probably wouldn't do it." Smoke caught her look of distress and laughed. "I'm joking. You'll be perfectly safe."

"Then why can't you tell me?"

"Why would I go to all this trouble of protecting you—risking my own neck, I might add—if I was just going to lead you to a horrible fate?"

Alys hesitated. He had a point. "You could be some kind of crazy person."

"Maybe," Smoke said. "But for all you know, this could all be a dream and it's you who is crazy."

"You said I wasn't dreaming."

"Yes, but if I am, in fact, part of that dream, what the hell would I know about it?"

Alys closed her mouth and thought on this a moment. He also had a point about that. The past few hours certainly had felt very dream-like—not like any dream she'd ever had, but still.

Smoke reached past her and opened the door, the light from inside casting a soft warm glow on his face as he gestured for her to enter first. "This will help protect you until we can get you back home, you have my word."

Alys stared at him a long moment before she took a hesitant step inside. Instantly, her whole body felt warm and comfortable, her fear and suspicion melting away. Within the building a strong blaze was crackling happily away inside an enormous fireplace. She smiled in spite of herself and stepped farther inside. She looked upward to see, much like she had in the Phrontistery, endless bookshelves stretching up and out of sight. Though, unlike the Phrontistery, a heavy layer of dust seemed to coat the shelves, and cobwebs hung from every nook and cranny. Some books looked new, while others were cracked at the spine with age. A handful were as thick as encyclopedias, and still others were as thin as paper slips. The only thing that any of the books had in common was that none of them seemed to be titled. "Curious," she murmured, reaching to take one off the shelf.

"Hello?" someone, a very old someone, called from the next room on the other side of several tall stacks of books that had yet to be re-shelved. "Who's out there?"

Alys startled a little. "Um...Alys?"

"Well, come in, come in where I can see you, goodness gracious," the voice called again.

Alys stepped forward, but looked back at Smoke, who hadn't moved and was busy examining books. "Are you coming?"

Smoke shook his head. "Nah. I think I'll do a bit of reading while I wait. You won't want me hanging about and eavesdropping anyway." He laughed at her uneasy expression. "I'll be right here. Go, go." He shooed her off before pulling one of the larger volumes off the shelf. "Remember, answer *every* question he asks."

Alys nodded and walked through the large archway that led into the next room. It looked much like the main room, circular, the walls lined with books, with others stacked in tall but neat piles she had to navigate around. Her eyes fell on the one big difference: A man was sitting at an impossibly large desk.

He was a frail-looking creature, and what little hair he had stuck straight out at his ears as if he'd slapped a bald cap over an otherwise full head of white hair. Perched on his buzzard-like nose was a pair of glasses so thick they magnified his eyes until they filled the entirety of the lenses. He was dressed in a black suit with a burgundy vest and wore a pleasant sort of smile.

"Do you have an appointment?" he asked cheerfully.

"Oh." Alys looked over her shoulder towards where she'd left Smoke in the other room. "I'm not entirely sure, actually. I don't think so?"

"Good." The man sounded almost relieved. "I would never have remembered it." He chuckled a little at this and settled in his seat, folding his hands on the desktop.

Alys smiled and looked down at the brass name plate resting at the front of his desk. "Ah, so you're Mr. Smith."

"Am I?" The man blinked, taking a moment to look at his surroundings. "Oh! Yes, of course I am. Of course I am, indeed." He tapped his nameplate importantly with his index finger.

"Um, a man by the name of Smoke sent me to see you?"

"A recommendation," Mr. Smith said in awe. "How unusual. We do good work here, but people seldom remember to tell anyone about it."

"Do you know him?"

"It's hard to remember what or who I know," Mr. Smith said, taking out a quill and ink. "So much information going in and out day after day. The mind does not know what to keep track of. Occupational hazard, I'm afraid." He paused a moment, completely still. His brow furrowed in concentration for a moment before relaxing. "I've forgotten what I was doing."

"I was recommended to come here and answer some questions for you," Alys offered.

"Ah! Good." Mr. Smith snapped his fingers and seemed to recall why he'd pulled out the quill and ink in the first place. "Now, do you have an account with us? With me? With us?" He paused and looked around, then leaned forward with a whisper. "Do I have any business partners?"

"I don't know." Alys gave a helpless smile.

"Neither do I!" he laughed. "I suppose that means I do this all on my own. Nasty thought. I should think I'd get quite lonely if I didn't keep forgetting I was by myself." He reached into another drawer and pulled out a thin hardcover book that appeared to have no more than three pages inside. "Sit, sit." He motioned her toward a large red plush wing-back on the opposite side of the desk.

Alys did as she was asked, but it required a bit of a hop and then some scooting until she was comfortable. Her feet didn't even come close to reaching the floor. She kicked them a little, feeling as if she'd suddenly shrunk down a few sizes again.

Mr. Smith propped the book up on a stand as if he was going to read from it, dipped the quill in the ink, and placed it to the page. "Now, then." He squinted in thought. "Where shall we start? At the very beginning?"

"Sure." Alys shrugged.

"Very well. And, remember, we'll start at the beginning and go on until you've reached the end. Then stop. It's very important we don't go past the end."

Alys blinked.

"Name?"

"Alyson Carroll."

The feather plume on the quill swayed as it wrote on the page.

"And your parents?"

"Lucy Carroll and…" Alys trailed off. "Well, I don't actually know. He left when I was really little. Mom didn't really talk about him much except to…" She looked away and then back again with a sheepish smile. "Well, anyway, I don't know anything about him."

Mr. Smith bobbed his head. "Quite all right, quite all right. That just makes our job easier."

Alys wanted to ask how any of this was helpful, but she wasn't the person asking questions here, and the last time she accidentally went against Smoke's instructions, things had ended far too unpleasantly. She could still hear the shrieks of The Nothing wailing in her ears. She shivered. Best to just follow his advice this time.

"Your place of birth?" She noticed his hands were now folded on the desk, and that the quill appeared to be writing on its own while he merely supervised its progress.

"Appleweed, Washington."

"Any siblings?"

"No."

"Tell me about your mother."

Alys drew her knees to her chest and wrapped her arms around them. Her gut churned.

"Is this something you want to keep?"

She *would* have preferred to keep it to herself, but Smoke had said to answer *every question*. And so she was going to answer *every question*. "My mother didn't grow up well. I suppose it makes sense that I didn't, either. Her father was an abusive alcoholic and..." She took a deep breath. "Well...I guess she just picked up the tradition, you know?"

Mr. Smith didn't comment.

She sank back into herself, trying to forget he was there. Reluctantly, she described their relationship—if that word was even appropriate to use. Alys tripped over the many nights she'd hidden under her bed from her mother or one of her overnight guests. She carefully picked around the feeling of cigarette burns, and hand-shaped bruises, and nearly threw up remembering the pungent smell of cheap vodka. She told him everything from a drunken jealous rage that resulted in her mother violently taking scissors to her hair when she was a child to recently having to hide her tip money so Lucy didn't steal it. She told him about the roses, about coming home and seeing white blooms where they'd been promised crimson. She told him about the absolute panic of being a seven-year-old girl trying to use watercolor paints to fix them, and the way the thorns bit her every time she got too close to the flowers. She told him about how the roses made her bleed, and then how her mother did.

"It's funny," Alys finished, realizing that at some point she'd started crying. She wiped at her eyes discreetly with her fingertips as if she was hoping Mr. Smith hadn't noticed. "I've never told anyone. Well, except Charlie, I guess…"

Mr. Smith looked up from his quill supervision, and, for the first time, his brow knit in concern. "Do you *want* to tell me about Charlie?"

There wasn't much of a hesitation this time, and Alys nodded. There was no turning back now, and at least for the most part, Charlie was a happy memory.

"Charlie is...*was* my best friend. He passed away yesterday. I think. I'm not really sure how long I've been here. Charlie and I met in second grade when his family moved into town. He was this scrawny little blond kid, and the moment he showed up, you knew there was something different about him. I don't mean the gay thing. I mean, there was just something in his eyes. Everyone else just assumed he was weird, but..." Her mouth twitched into a sad, knowing smile. "But I knew that look too well to dismiss it so easily." She started to focus on her nails as she picked intently at her cuticles. "Honestly, Charlie and I became friends because we were both damaged people. We knew what it was like to have scars you couldn't talk about." Her breath shuddered. "But it became so much more than that, you know? We were family. Real family."

The quill had resumed its dance, and she vaguely noticed that the book looked thicker now. Despite the fact that it had started with only three pages, as each page turned so the writing could begin anew, there was always a fresh one waiting on the other side.

And so she told him about Charlie and their similar parenting experience. She explained about Charles Lewis Senior's temper, and Karen Lewis's kind heart that was regretfully too petrified to do anything for either her son or herself. She talked about Mr. Lewis's gun cabinet and intentions of sending Charlie to West Point. She talked about Charlie's depression, and his strange battle between wanting to get better, and not looking weak in the eyes of his father. And then she talked about happier things because they were easier, like Brian and Seattle, and trips out of Appleweed – the plans that they would never follow through with. She talked about school and the days he'd visited Susie's Diner to keep her company on weekends. She excitedly recounted late night movie-marathons, explorations into the forest surrounding Appleweed, and the dilapidated fort they'd made when they were thirteen. She talked about the hornets' nest that nested there and had drove them out, and Brian's eventual graduation. She talked about the stone steps she and Charlie retreated to. She talked about the countless games of chess. She described the last time she'd seen him, and that nothing seemed out of the ordinary. She insisted to Mr. Smith that Charlie had given her no indication of what he'd decided to do that night.

Sometimes she spoke on her own, and sometimes Mr. Smith guided her with questions, but they continued on about her life, covering every intimate to mundane detail. She tried to remain as linear as possible, but, often, as she was reminded of something, she'd skip around to talk about things that seemed relevant.

It felt like days had passed.

He asked her about Appleweed, and she told him about Susie, her diner, and Mary Ann. She talked about how mold grew everywhere if you turned your back for too long. She related trudging from kindergarten to high school graduation: all she could remember of her lessons, her teachers, and any anecdote that cropped up. She spoke about everything she could think of, and the quill seemed to scrawl her answers into the book with a speed that stayed only a breath behind her words as if it was anticipating them. The book filled with more and more pages, stuffed with her knowledge of geography and literature—even lyrics and tunes to any song she'd ever memorized or even vaguely knew.

And just as her voice was getting hoarse and it seemed as if they'd exhausted every question she could possibly answer, the quill stopped moving.

Mr. Smith returned the quill to the ink-well for the first time and adjusted his glasses. Peering at the pages before nodding in satisfaction, he pulled it from the stand to hand it to her with great effort. "Here."

Alys scooted forward quickly to take it from him, mainly because it had grown so large and he looked so frail and shaky beneath its weight. She held it to her chest to support the heavy thing and looked to Mr. Smith, who looked at her rather expectantly. "What?"

"Aren't you going to read it?"

Alys looked down at the book. She was sure she knew exactly what was in it, as she'd been the one who'd provided the content. Still, she decided to humor him and leaned back in the chair. She rubbed her eyes and opened to the first page.

It was blank.

She looked up at Mr. Smith, who just smiled at her. Then she glanced back down at the page, her brow furrowing as she looked to the next page. Again, blank.

Her head was starting to ache.

She flipped back to the first page and saw words beginning to seep through the paper as if an ink spill had occurred beneath them. Her eyes widened a little as she scanned over them. It was all there, forming as she read from page to page until it retold everything from being lost in Thought and her encounter with The Nothing and Charlie, until, finally, walking into the very office she now currently sat.

Alys closed the book and stared at the back cover thoughtfully, feeling absolutely exhausted.

"Was it a good book?" Smoke draped himself over the back of the wingback chair. He held his hand out for it.

She surrendered the book to him with a shrug. "I don't really remember."

"Couldn't have been that important, then," Smoke offered, tucking it under his arm.

"No." Alys rubbed her eyes. "I suppose not." She looked at Smoke as he came around to her side, giving him an up and down sort of glance before her gaze rested on his face. "Who are you?"

Smoke grinned. "Just a friend."

Chapter 11

FINDING ALYS

Oswin was admittedly tired by the time the small party emerged from the Tulgey Wood. He'd had little rest since his escape, but, while his body longed for sleep, he knew that would be far off. Even with Oswin's recollections and Smoke's sense of direction, they'd managed to get lost more than once and had had to make camp for a few hours to regain their strength. He'd never been so relieved to see his cousin's home.

Untimely Manor resided on the very edge of Thought, and while it was grand and rather obvious once you did find it, it always took a bit of aimless wandering to get to it.

Robin took point while Basir lagged behind, keeping a close eye on Oswin as if he was worried the younger man would collapse at any minute. After they'd parted ways with Smoke and Jack near the door to The Nothing, they'd spoken little. With one man less, Robin had taken to being extra watchful and insisting they remain quiet to not draw attention to themselves.

As they approached the manor, Robin dropped back to allow Oswin to pass her and knock on the door. "Rosalind?" He paused and looked back at his two advisors. "I hope she's all right."

"By my calculations, Your Highness," Basir assured him, "it's highly improbable The Nightmare's army has extended their reach this far. Her resources are still limited to Elan Vital."

"I'd also like to remind you that this isn't the first war Rosalind has gone through. It wouldn't be this picturesque if the Nightmare had beaten us here," said Robin.

The door opened, but no one was expecting the woman they saw on the other side.

"Mary Ann?"

Alys smiled at him a little blankly, tilting her head to the side. She peered at them curiously but said nothing.

"What are you doing here?"

Alys opened her mouth to answer but stopped and furrowed her brow. She didn't have an answer for that. She looked like she was trying to solve an incredibly complicated math problem.

"Your Highness?" Basir asked Oswin cautiously. "Who is this?"

"This is Mary Ann, the girl from earlier," Oswin explained quickly to his companions, which caused Robin to raise her eyebrows and Basir's back to stiffen. He turned back to Alys incredulously. "How…how did you get here?"

"Oh." Alys looked suddenly relieved. Something she *did* know the answer to. "I walked!"

"Can we come in?" Robin asked, looking over her shoulder again almost nervously.

"Oh, yes, of course." Alys nodded, stopped as if remembering something, and then asked, "Who are you?"

"Introductions, sorry," Oswin apologized, gesturing to his two companions, who didn't really see this as being the time for formalities. "Mary Ann, this is Robin and Basir, my mother, the late queen's, Rhyme and Reason."

Alys nodded again, but his explanation obviously hadn't cleared up any of her confusion. She looked to Oswin. "And you are?"

Oswin's brow furrowed. "Mary Ann, it's me. Oswin. We met—"

"Was that the door?" A beautiful dark-skinned woman gently pushed Alys aside so she could get a look at the guests herself. Nobility, to be sure, she wore a soft golden gown which framed her neck and collarbone and fanned out at her hips in a full skirt. A collar independent from the dress was fastened at her neck, giving her a lace trim around her throat not unlike an Elizabethan ruff. She was of average height, but still stood nearly a full head taller than Alys. Her features were striking, with a strong jawline and high cheekbones that were only further accentuated by the wild, natural curls that fell past her shoulders.

"Rosalind, it's so good to see you again." Oswin took a step forward to embrace his cousin, who returned the gesture tightly.

"Come inside, quickly," Rosalind said. "Not even Thought is safe these days from prying eyes."

Alys closed the door behind them as they moved into the grand foyer, Basir giving her an unsure look as he passed.

"I was so worried." Rosalind led them down the hallway to the study. "When I heard you escaped to the Other Side, I didn't know what to think."

"It threw them off my trail." Oswin glanced over his shoulder at Alys, who was lagging behind because she kept staring at anything her eyes could rest on. The intricate threading of the carpets, the high ceilings, the painting on the walls—it was all fascinating to her. "Rosalind…how did *she* get here?" He dropped his voice like he was suddenly worried Alys would hear him.

"Silas brought her." Rosalind gestured for them all to take a seat and rest their feet. "Can I get anyone anything? Tea or soup?" She stopped suddenly, looking at them as a whole. "You're one less than when you left."

Oswin eyed her with confusion. "Who's Silas?"

"Smoke," Robin clarified for Oswin as she sat before turning back to Rosalind. "Is he here? Last we saw him he was with my brother, investigating the door."

"Why are you calling Smoke Silas?" The prince was having trouble getting off the subject.

"It's his name," Rosalind answered defensively, managing a shake of the head at Robin's question.

"No, it isn't!" Oswin insisted, and then looked to Robin for clarification. "Is it?"

Robin nodded.

"Well, how come he didn't tell me that?"

Robin looked away like she was either biting her tongue or trying not to laugh. Possibly both.

Basir just shook his head at Oswin, assuring him he probably wouldn't have liked the answer if he knew it anyway.

At this point, Alys had made her way to the doorway of the study. She put her hands in her pockets as she had so many times before in idleness, and while the action was ingrained in her muscle memory, for her freshly cleared brain, it was a completely new experience. She was elated and surprised and even a little confused at this new discovery, then even more so when she realized there was something *inside* her pocket. She pulled out a crumpled piece of paper and carefully unfolded it with great reverence. The words she found on it further bewildered her as they were now completely without context. Without knowledge of any social graces, she interrupted the conversation without consideration. "Are any of you Alys?"

The group looked at her as if they had forgotten there was a Dreamer among them. They remained still as if worried any sudden noise or movement might incite some terrible action from her, but said nothing.

Alys returned their blank expressions and held up the paper as if it would explain everything. "I think I'm supposed to give her a message." She looked to each of them, then shrugged when she received no answer. "No bother. I'll go look for her." She exited the study and started back down the hallway.

"There's something not quite right about that one," Basir said as pleasantly as he could manage.

"She wasn't like this when I met her," Oswin said defensively, turning to Rosalind. "Is she all right? Was she injured? She doesn't seem to have a clue who I am."

Rosalind shook her head. "She's been like that since they got here."

"What did he do?"

"Whatever he had to do, I imagine," Basir said under his breath.

"I don't know what you think you're implying…" Smoke was sitting on the sill of an open window, one leg still dangling outside from when he'd silently climbed through it, a thick leather-bound book tucked under his arm. "…but the insinuation is far from flattering, Master Reason. I assure you, I didn't touch a hair on her head."

"Are you completely incapable of making your presence known without eavesdropping for a few minutes first?" Basir huffed.

Smoke stood up and took a genuine pause to think about it as he closed the window behind him. "You know? I don't believe I've ever tried."

"What's that?" Oswin asked suspiciously, pointing to the book.

"Her memories," Smoke answered, dropping it onto the table with a loud thud. "Seems like she wandered into the Office of Oblivion, and not understanding the gist of the place, accidentally surrendered every recollection over to their archive. I went back and graciously recovered them for her."

The Prince wasn't so easily convinced of Smoke's innocence in the matter. "How did she get there?"

Smoke met the other man's look firmly. "Maybe you should ask her. How would I know?"

"Is my brother with you?"

Smoke hesitated before looking at Robin. "We were separated."

Robin frowned. "What do you mean, you were separated?"

"The Nightmare has soldiers patrolling the Tulgey Wood now. We split up to lose them, but Jack never showed up at The Door."

"So where the hell is he, then?"

"I don't know," Smoke answered quietly.

A tense silence fell over the room as Robin rose from her chair. "You just left him?"

"I couldn't waste time looking for him, Robin. I had to find the Dreamer."

"They know his face, Silas. They know what he's done. He's wanted for treason. If that *thing* gets a hold of him, he'll die!"

"If *that thing* gets a hold of the Dreamer, *we all die!*" Smoke's eyes narrowed. "She wouldn't need to corrupt any more dreams, Robin. She could make her own damned army of Nightmares. We're lucky the girl hasn't managed to *damage Terra Mirum on her own*, let alone fallen into the wrong hands."

Robin remained silent for a few moments, looking off to the side obstinately. She couldn't really argue with Smoke's reasoning, but she didn't have to like it, either. "I'm going to go look for him," she finally stated.

"Be my guest."

She raised her chin defiantly and looked around at the others, furious that no one seemed to share her anger. She looked to Basir, but he said nothing. "Fine." She turned on her heel, practically leaving a trail of fire in her wake, the front door slamming behind her.

"She has a right to be angry," Oswin finally said once the bang of the door stopped resonating.

"What would you have had me do, Your Highness?" Smoke demanded. "Jack is a trained soldier. I figured he could, at the very least, defend himself."

"It's just...I owe him my life. I don't think I could have dismissed possibly saving his so easily."

Smoke looked at him, but rather than raising his voice as he clearly wanted to, he spoke very softly. "You have yet to take the throne, Your Highness, so let me educate you on a very simple but difficult lesson every leader has to learn at one point or another: You don't get to save everyone. I took a gamble on the chance that, if caught, he'd be able to get out of it. Let's not linger on the morality of the decision. Let's just hope I was right." He took a deep breath. "Now, where is the Dreamer?"

"She went to go look for someone named Alys," Basir murmured, rubbing his face, feeling stubble growing in after a day's neglect.

Smoke blinked. "She *is* Alys."

"No, her name is Mary Ann," Oswin answered.

Smoke snorted. "Mary Ann? *Really*? No, I don't think so."

"You're not doing well with names today, are you?" Rosalind asked sympathetically.

"She told me her name was Mary Ann," Oswin insisted, feeling a little defensive now.

"Well, she lied," Smoke said. "Don't look so betrayed. I probably wouldn't want to tell some strange man I met in a train tunnel my real name either, if I was her."

Oswin huffed a little and stood. "I'll go get her."

Chapter 12

MYTH AND MEMORY

Alys wandered upstairs and was doing an excellent job of getting herself absolutely lost in the manor. She'd been unable to find another soul for the longest time until she entered one of the larger bedrooms.

A girl on the other side of the room startled, staring back at her with wide eyes as if she, too, had been convinced she was completely alone upstairs. She looked pale, even with all the lights out, and as Alys approached her, she could see they were roughly the same height.

The other girl had pulled her dark hair back into a loose ponytail. She had light scratches on her hands and face and dirt on her sweatshirt. Both she and the ponytail had seen better days, and looked like they'd gone through quite a bit in the past few hours.

Alys attempted a smile, and the girl timidly returned it. "Are you Alys?"

The girl didn't answer, but as Alys met the other girl's sad brown eyes, she felt her heart wrench.

Her fingers trembled as she unfolded the small scrap of paper again. "Charlie says he's sorry," Alys whispered. The words caught in her throat and she trembled.

The other girl's eyes looked glassy and, as she looked about to cry, Alys felt her own eyes welling up with tears.

She couldn't explain why, but something about hearing herself saying those words and seeing how it hurt the other girl was unbearably heartbreaking. Tears streamed down the other girl's dirty cheeks, and Alys covered her own face with her hands, thinking if she didn't look at the upset girl, she might be able to stop crying herself. But she couldn't. She choked and shook, and she sank down to a crouch and wrapped her arms around herself, the note still clutched in her hands.

"Alys?" Oswin called quietly from the doorway.

The other girl wiped at her eyes in embarrassment and Alys turned to see who was coming just in time to see Oswin enter.

The prince frowned a little upon seeing her expression. "Hey," he said, approaching her with absolute caution. "Are you okay?"

Alys slowly stood, absently wiping at her eyes. "I don't know. I—I was just trying to deliver a message for Charlie and…"

"Who is Charlie?"

Alys cried harder. "I don't know! I had this note." She held it out to him and then gestured to the other girl, who pointed back in accusation. "And I tried to tell her, and she got upset and started crying, and then *I* started crying."

Oswin took the note, read it, and looked from her to the girl that Alys had indicated, then to the note again and back to Alys before pocketing the note. "Alys, that's a mirror."

"What?" Alys turned back to see a perfect copy of Oswin's likeness had now joined the girl she'd been speaking to. She raised a hand and watched the girl mimic her gesture. She then raised it to her face, slowly massaging her face with her fingertips before looking back at him. "Is that what I look like?"

Oswin smiled a little and gently raised a hand to her cheek, brushing away both dirt and tears with his thumb. "Yeah…"

"Am *I* Alys?"

He nodded. "I think so."

"I can't…I can't remember," Alys sniffled.

"I know," he said. "We're going to help you."

"I know I knew who I was when I got up this morning," Alys insisted. "At least, I think I did. I feel like so much has changed since then."

"It really has." Oswin thought about his own journey since he was pulled from his bed late at night. "Can you come downstairs? I think we have something that will sort all of this out."

"Really?"

"Really."

"How?"

"You'll just have to trust me." He held out his hand to her, lightly wiggling his fingers and giving her a reassuring smile.

Without memory to jade the concept, she nodded and took his hand. And for the first time, Alys just trusted someone.

***

"We're sure we have the right book?" Oswin asked Smoke as he returned to the library, leading an amnesiac Alys gently by the hand.

"Absolutely," Smoke answered with all sincerity. "It took a lot of work, but I'm certain this is the book we need." He pulled out a chair at the table so Alys could sit.

"Book?" Alys looked at it, bewildered.

"Yes," Smoke said. "This is called a book."

"I hope she can still remember how to read," Basir said.

Oswin glared at his own advisor and motioned for Alys to take the chair. "Trust me, once you read it, you'll be your old self in no time."

Alys sat and looked at the large book in front of her, unable to understand how a book would help, or why their tone of voice made her feel so stupid. "You want me to read this?" She asked Smoke, acknowledging the book's great size. "All of this?"

"Don't worry," Smoke assured her. "Remembering is a lot easier than forgetting; you'll buzz right through it."

Alys hadn't the slightest idea what he meant by that, but she still nodded and pulled open the cover. "Alyson Carroll," she read aloud. She blinked. "That's my name!" She looked at Smoke, then Oswin, then Basir and Rosalind, her face beaming with pride as the euphoria of remembering something you'd been desperate to recall hit her.

"Keep going." Smoke patted her shoulder. "To yourself."

Alys nodded and winced a little, muttering an apology before looking back down at the book, her eyes rapidly scanning down the page before turning it.

Oswin watched her suspiciously for a moment as he observed something. "Is that book missing pages? It looks like quite a few were ripped out." He pointed to frayed paper edges sticking out of the binding.

"The book was damaged," Smoke said. "But it's not short any pages, if that's what you're worried about."

Oswin nodded, but found himself still watching as Alys read through one of the loose papers, turning it over before placing it down and moving on to the next page.

"We need a plan," Smoke began, leaning against one of the tables. "The castle is likely completely impenetrable now, and we have no way to get to the Nightmare."

"Or my father," Oswin added, folding his arms as he remembered the lifeless puppet that had doggedly followed the Nightmare around that night. Hardly even a shadow of the man he'd once been, and no longer a king of any kind.

"I've been doing some research," Rosalind piped up. "Outside the Phrontistery, there isn't much recorded history on dealing with Nightmares, but there is some—older texts, mind you—mostly reduced to legend."

Oswin looked doubtful. "You're referring to the legend of the Jabberwock?"

Rosalind nodded. "I am."

"With all due respect, Your Grace," Basir began slowly. "The slaying of the Jabberwock is just a myth. A story we tell our children to inspire courage."

Rosalind shook her head. "The myth is what we all know, but it's actually based on a battle from as far back as when The Nothing was first created to separate Dream from Nightmare."

"So you're suggesting we defeat this Nightmare using what? A vorpal blade?" The Queen's Reason tried his best to remain polite and not too skeptical. Rosalind was still nobility.

"Precisely," Rosalind answered levelly.

"It's ridiculous."

"Basir," Oswin warned.

"Your Grace, forgive me for speaking so plainly. I mean no disrespect, but the very idea that our only hope is couched in fairytale is unacceptable. We need an army. We need a strategy. Not a weapon that may or may not even exist outside of poetry."

"Vorpal blades *do* exist," Rosalind said.

"What's a vorpal blade?" Alys asked, directing her attention to her. The book in front of her was closed. "It sounds really familiar."

Oswin eyed the book. "You finished all of that?"

"Yeah," Alys answered, a little surprised herself. "It was weird…like…all I had to do was turn a page and I knew what was on it." She looked at Smoke. "Is that how it's supposed to happen? Also, my head really hurts."

"Do you remember why you went to the

Office of Oblivion in the first place?" Smoke asked carefully.

Alys thought a moment and shook her head. "Not really. I remember…getting lost in Thought. I think I just…wandered in, and then he just started asking me all these questions so…I guess it seemed rude not to answer."

Smoke nodded and patted her shoulder. "You're not the first, trust me."

Alys looked at him, her eyes squinting almost suspiciously before saying, "Don't do that—it's patronizing." She turned back around. "Okay, bear with me. I think I have a lot of catching up to do, and I think having all my memories returned at once may have triggered a migraine." She began to work out the situation with gestures, indicating loca- tions in the air around her to represent Earth and Terra Mirum. "This is essentially what people from my world, or whatever, call 'the dream world,' yes? Like this is where our consciousness goes when we sleep?"

The group looked at each other before nodding. That was the gist, more or less.

"We call it Terra Mirum," Oswin offered.

Alys nodded and motioned dismissively to what had become 'her world' in her gesticulations, then back to her current location. "But I'm not in my world, asleep. I'm actually here?"

"Correct," Smoke answered with a crooked grin.

"And it's been taken over because this thing that was let out of a place you call 'The Nothing,' which is basically where all the bad things that humans have ever imagined are locked up."

"Basically," Oswin confirmed.

"This is a lot to take in, in one go." Alys blinked a little and leaned back.

"We don't have a lot of time," Basir said.

"Just give me a minute, okay?" Alys asked. "I'm getting there." She took a deep breath and continued talking herself through the logic. "I walked into the office of some kooky old man, and, apparently, just by answering his questions, I lost all ability to remember who I am, where I'm from, and everything in between. And, had it not been for you lot, I would still be wandering around, not even recognizing my own reflection? Am I correct so far?"

"Yeah…" Oswin seemed a little embarrassed for her.

"And, by the look of all the guards swarming the entrance when I got here…I'm not likely going to be able to go home until this is all over?"

"Uhh…" Oswin looked to Basir, who shook his head grimly. "Probably not, no…"

"Okay," Alys spoke levelly and folded her hands in her lap. "In that case, how can I help?"

Smoke smiled, but the others looked surprised and taken aback by this offer.

"You…want to help us?" Basir asked.

"Well, yeah," Alys offered, smiling a little. "Who knows what would have happened to me without Smoke's help, so I feel I kinda owe you guys big time. Plus, it's not like I have any other options. Can't exactly go home with the creepy tin soldiers blocking my way, now can I? I mean, I could just sit around here and wait, but that seems rather counterproductive."

"You realize you're signing up for something incredibly dangerous here," Oswin stated, giving her an incredulous eye. However, unlike their first encounter, there appeared to be no sarcasm in her voice. The woman before him was the absolute picture of sincerity. He crouched down beside her chair so he didn't feel like he was literally talking down to her. "We're talking about a war, Alys. People will die."

Alys nodded. "A war that now includes me, Oswin. I mean, what's going to happen to me if you lose? What's going to happen to Earth? Besides, if I remember correctly, it wasn't exactly a picnic trying to help me, either."

"Interesting…" Rosalind murmured, looking at Alys in reverent wonder.

"What is?" Oswin looked from Alys to his cousin.

"It's just…" Rosalind slid into the seat opposite Alys, peering at her as if she could draw out some kind of tell that the girl across the table was bluffing. She found nothing. "A vorpal blade is created only when a great Fear has been overcome. It is literally forged by the defeat of a Nightmare."

"Then how are we supposed to even find one?" Basir asked, exasperated.

Rosalind continued as if she'd never heard him. "And a vorpal weapon can only be wielded by the courageous — by someone not ruled by fear." She looked back at Smoke. "Did you plan this?"

Smoke looked back at her, his face unchanging. "Plan what, my dear?"

Rosalind looked back at Alys, and then Oswin. "Cousin, I think we found the one person who may truly be able to wield the vorpal blade."

Oswin pursed his lips as he looked at Alys, bewildered.

Alys nodded with the lack of worry one might have after they'd realized they were in a dream and nothing could harm them. "Awesome. Let's do this."

"Do you even know how to use a sword?" Oswin asked.

"Well — " Alys was about to deny that she did, but then she remembered reading — no, remembered *doing*--something. "Of...course I do." It was coming back to her rapidly, the weight of a blade in her hand, hours of practice against dummies day and night. Her determination to rise in the ranks and stand out among the other recruits. She stumbled over it, confused. It was a strange memory that didn't seem to fit with any of the rest, yet there it was in her brain as clear as the taste of ice cream or the walk between her house and Charlie's.

Charlie.

She remembered who Charlie was, and it made her heart simultaneously flutter and ache, but she couldn't explain why. *Wait.* She thought of the note. Why was Charlie sorry?

"Look," Basir sighed, standing. "Whether she can or can't, we seem to be forgetting that we have no way of getting a vorpal blade. The Nightmare has not been vanquished. Are you even listening to yourselves? You can't defeat something with a weapon that requires you to defeat it first to obtain it—that's not possible!"

The front door burst open and Robin entered from the foyer, out of breath and covered in scratches from a less than graceful navigation through the woods. "They have him," she breathed. "Those bastards took Jack."

Chapter 13

PAINTING THE ROSES RED

"You're sure?" Oswin asked gravely.

"I saw them." Robin was still out of breath. "Nearly a whole squad of guards, armed to the teeth—you'd think the war was still going on. There were too many. I couldn't stop them."

"Don't blame yourself." Basir stood to embrace her, but she would have none of it. She pushed him away, maneuvering out of his arms.

"We don't have much time. They'll already have a great start on us. We need to move quickly."

"Move quickly...to do what, exactly?" Smoke asked carefully.

"Rescue him," Robin spat incredulously.

"They're taking him to the palace He doesn't stand a chance!"

"And if we go charging after him, neither will we," Smoke answered calmly.

"So you're saying we should do nothing?"

"I'm saying we should continue with the plan."

"The plan?" Robin asked skeptically.

"*The Duchess* believes a vorpal blade is the key to destroying the Nightmare," Basir said.

Robin narrowed her eyes as she turned around. "I don't see how that would prevent us from helping my brother."

"We don't have time—" Smoke started.

"Exactly, Silas, we *don't* have time. That's my point! They will take him back to that *thing,* and after she has drained everything she can from him, *she will kill him.*"

"Robin—"

"You have to get inside the palace to get your stupid blade anyway. Why the hell can't we save one of our own while we're at it?" Venom rose in the Fae's voice.

"Wait," Oswin said, his attention focusing in a pinpoint on Robin. "Are you saying the vorpal blade has been in the palace this whole time? You're sure?"

"Your Highness, I was the Queen's Rhyme long before you were even conceived. Don't insult me by questioning my knowledge." Robin's lip curled.

"You're saying a vorpal blade actually exists?" Basir dropped his jaw.

"The blade has been passed down in the royal family for years." Robin shook her head in disbelief that no one else knew what she had considered to be common knowledge. "Long ago, as legend tells, when Nightmares roamed Thought and beyond, Morpheus, only a young prince then, rose against the strongest of the creatures. Jabberwock, they called it. And from his courage there was forged a blade far stronger than any steel, and with it did he lob off the head of the beast and seal the Nightmares behind a great door, leaving them imprisoned to the will of mortal thought. And since that battle, the blade has taken part in every subsequent coronation ceremony to remind Terra Mirum's ruler to be constantly vigilant. That the door must never open again." She looked to Oswin. "I'm surprised you weren't aware of this, Your Highness."

The prince looked a little embarrassed. "I was aware of the legend—just not its connection to my family. When I was reading about the coronation, I assumed it was purely symbolic, not the actual sword itself."

Rosalind brought her hand to her lips, averting her eyes suddenly as if a thought had struck her, but only Alys noticed her concern. The Duchess turned slightly, looking back towards one of the shelves near the back of the room.

"Even still, we need a plan," Smoke reasoned. "We can't go charging into the palace. That's suicide."

"Look," Robin started again. "I'm going to help my brother, with or without you. He wouldn't even be involved in this mess if it wasn't for me, and I will not abandon him now. Consider me the distraction that will make way for you to reach the palace treasury."

"I'm afraid I have to agree with Silas," Rosalind answered. "What we do now is crucial. If we're too hasty, we could lose everything."

Robin was out of patience, and she spun on her heel to storm out, but Basir caught her arm. For a moment, Robin looked like she might be ready to turn and strike him. "*Let me go.*"

"I'm going with you," Basir answered. He offered a small, unsure smile.

Robin smiled back, looking relieved that she could still count on him, if no one else.

"Wait," Oswin sighed, moving past Smoke. "I'm going, too."

"Oswin," Rosalind protested.

"The man saved my life, Rosalind. The least I could do is attempt to return the favor."

"I'm going too!" Alys stood with the bounce and easiness as if someone had merely suggested they all take a trip to the store. She again drew looks of disbelief. She blinked. "What? I want to help."

"*You* are definitely not going," Smoke protested.

Alys looked at him curiously as she moved to join the group. "Why not? I'm not afraid. I don't know the meaning of the word." Unbeknownst to her, she truly didn't.

Smoke looked to every face in the small party for some support.

"If you're so worried," Robin started, "come with us."

Smoke growled in frustration. "This is a huge mistake." He started towards them, but stopped as he passed Rosalind, who was standing up from her chair. He took her hands in his and kissed both sets of knuckles. "We'll be back."

Rosalind ignored the look Oswin gave her at this interaction. "If you manage to get the blade, come back and we'll regroup. But, please, promise me you won't do anything stupid. I'll try to find out more, if I can — anything. "

"I have a bad feeling about all this," the man muttered.

Rosalind kissed his forehead. "Just be careful."

***

The city of Elan Vital had, at one point, been a great metropolis, but today the streets were barren and quiet. The group wandered in cautiously, unable to shake the knowledge that they were walking right into the Nightmare Queen's hand.

"Where is everyone?" Alys asked, and Oswin hushed her.

Robin stopped and angled her head slightly, leaning forward like an animal hearing something in the distance. Her ears twitched a little. "I think I can hear someone talking — loudly."

Smoke bent forward in a smooth motion, wisps of vapor curling around him until, in his place, stood a large jungle cat of indeterminable breed. It was lean and striped, its ears seemed more proportioned to that of a house cat, and, while it was common knowledge in the group that it was merely their friend in another form, it looked disturbingly feral. His ears perked up and he looked back at the group. "They're in the gardens."

Oswin didn't see the significance. "The royal gardens?"

Robin paled a little. "It's a wide open space." There was a grim realization to her voice that everyone except Alys seemed to understand.

Basir shifted his coat to the side and placed his hand on the hilt of his rapier. "We're with you," he murmured reassuringly.

It was the only encouragement Robin needed to run ahead, leading the group down the city's Main Street towards the royal palace. A dark cloud seemed to hang over everything, the sky seemingly devoid of sunlight as if it was afraid to tread anywhere near the place.

They slowed as they reached the palace entrance to the garden and the hedge pathways that lead up to the great castle itself. Alys could hear what Robin and Smoke had heard before. A woman's voice. They wound around the corner, and the hollow quality of the voice resonated in her chest uncomfortably. It made her pulse shudder and blood hum.

"And as for Aislynn, your dear sovereign's death, you bear your minds in grief, and hearts in woe."

They were getting closer now, and, with the final turn of the winding paths, the hedge gave way to a great space where the people had gathered in utter, terrified silence.

A great white marble platform had been constructed years ago during the palace's infancy, and its main occupation had been to lift performers above the ground to entertain the court so even the smallest lady's maid had perfect view. A ring of roses wrapped around the perimeter of the platform, and Alys noticed the flowers seemed to be everywhere. They intermingled with the hedges, they were carved into the marble itself, and they even seemed to bloom from the trees that outlined the courtyard. Though strange, were the circumstances different, it would have been a beautiful sight.

But today the platform had a darker employment, supporting a woman who seemed to be woven from shadow itself. She addressed the crowd around the platform, which consisted of the entire city, and despite the great space, it was still far too tight a fit to offer any kind of comfortable view.

"Yet there are some who fight with nature's will," the woman continued. "And rather than with wisest sorrow grieve, they join in revolution for her name."

Alys could barely see anything, only

catching glimpses between people's heads if she craned her neck enough.

"Therefore, our appetite is fixed for blood, our armies resolve to this war-like state..."

Smoke materialized as his natural form next to Alys, his eyes trained on Robin, whose eyes were desperately searching the crowd.

Alys could not get a good look at the woman's face, but caught glimpses of her silhouette, from the black, clinging fabric to the tall, web-like collar that fanned out behind her head. "Who is that?" Alys whispered softly to Oswin, feeling an icy chill reverberating down her spine. She took Oswin's hand in her own.

Oswin's mouth was set in a grim, straight line. "The Nightmare."

"And we..." the Nightmare reached out her hand and Alys could see an old, tired looking man shakily reaching to take it. "... who shall not waver in our laws..." Decrepit seemed too generous an adjective to describe the man. "...with an auspicious and all-seeing eye..." The crown seemed to sit heavily on his head as if the sheer weight of the ornate structure would collapse his skull inward, and the irises of his eyes had paled so closely to white that he was undoubtedly blind.

"Who is that?" Alys whispered again.

Oswin grimaced. "My father."

"Does he always look like that?"

"...did pluck a rebel from his filthy cause..."

Oswin was about to turn an incredulous look on Alys for asking such a question, but, in doing so, caught sight of Robin, who was moving discreetly between the crowd, closer and closer to the platform. "Shit..."

Smoke followed Oswin's gaze and held out his hand to stop the prince from making his own advance, indicating that Basir was close behind her, and if any more followed, they'd draw attention to themselves.

"...to lay upon this altar here to die."

Guards held a man whose hands were shackled behind him. He had a sack over his head. They marched him from the crowd and onto the platform just before Robin managed to weave her way to them. She tried to continue, but was caught around the shoulders by her husband, who pulled her back into the anonymity of the crowd.

The guards, much like the King, looked on with dead eyes glazed over with a white sheen — as if they could not focus on anything around them, only stare ahead at something in the distance. They marched in perfect time, and Alys felt Oswin's hand around hers loosen.

Alys looked at the man at her side who had placed his fingers in his ears and seemed to be breathing imperfectly on purpose, breaking up the rhythm that the guards' feet had set. His eyes were closed tightly and he was bent over a little as if in pain. She set her hand on his back in concern, faintly feeling his heartbeat in the palm of her hand. Her lips pursed and she looked back up at the platform. Oswin's breathing was breaking up the rhythm, but, for just a moment, she could have sworn his heart had been beating in perfect time with the marching of their feet.

The guards placed their hands on their prisoner's shoulders, and he knelt without resistance or complaint before a large stone pedestal that seemed to have no place on the stage. It was far less well-kept, and may have once been the cornerstone to a now demolished building that someone had rescued from the debris for this ominous purpose.

From her place in the crowd, Alys could see the Nightmare's long, pale hand reaching down with almost claw-like fingers and pulling the sack from the man's head.

"Jack..." Smoke whispered.

Jack looked as lifeless as the rest of them, a moving, breathing body with no consciousness to fill it. A puppet to the Nightmare's whim.

"You're charged with treason and are deemed guilty. May others see your crimes and fear to tread, the path you took can bring nothing but death." The Nightmare turned to acknowledge the guards and nodded. "Soldiers, take up your arms."

Oswin dropped to a crouch, and Alys knelt with him, her brow furrowing in concern. "Oswin, what's—?"

"Off with his head."

The sound Alys heard was surreal, the kind of sound she'd never thought she'd hear outside a movie theater: the sound of a blade whistling through the air before searing through flesh. It took her a moment to understand exactly what had happened, but, as she looked towards the platform, she could see between the legs of the crowd and spotted the roses at the base. Red drops dripped and dribbled down the petals from the stage above, starting slow and gaining speed as the sheer volume of it increased.

Alys felt dizzy with nausea, the floral scent of the rose blooms seemingly overpowered by the smell of iron. Flashes of memories of trying to spread red color over white petals with a tiny paint brush stumbled through her mind. She blinked and looked away, her heart twisting painfully inside her.

In doing this, she could see Basir half-dragging Robin from the crowd, one hand clamped over her mouth and the other holding her tightly to him.

"This rebellion and its instigators, shall each receive the fate of this poor boy. We do not have the patience anymore. We have found the place where the rats do nest and set upon them even as We speak."

Smoke looked visibly disturbed and looked from Basir to Alys before sinking down back into the appearance of a cat and taking off as quickly as his legs would let him.

Alys helped Oswin stand, an arm around his waist while he leaned against her.

"Your queen is dead and none stand in Our way. All shall bow and submit to Our control."

Oswin flinched and turned his head inward towards Alys's neck, shaking.

"As for your valiant prince? So much for him."

Basir nodded towards the exit, and they both made their way as quickly and discreetly as possible out of sight and earshot.

Robin pulled away angrily, a guttural growl escaping her as she turned on him. "I trusted you."

"If you'd had any chance of saving him, Robin, believe me, I would have let you."

"He was right there, he was..." Robin's voice was weak, the execution playing over and over again in her thoughts in disturbing detail.

Basir closed his eyes and rested a hand on his wife's shoulder, knowing his next words would not be received well. "Robin, we're running out of time."

"No, Basir, we *never* had time. We were out of time when Aislynn was murdered. We've just been fooling ourselves."

Oswin was managing to stand on his own feet now, though he still seemed pale and unnerved by whatever had come over him minutes before, his voice breathless and raspy. "They're going after Rosalind."

Robin and Basir looked back at him.

"That's what she meant by finding the nest. It's why Smoke took off. They're going to Rosalind's."

Chapter 14

SHAKESPEARE, SWORDS, AND SOVEREIGNS

They smelled the fire before they could see it. The height of the trees and the thickness of their foliage had blocked the flood of smoke that was pouring out and up from the manor's windows.

Smoke himself was nowhere to be seen, but the front doors had been left wide open.

"Rosalind," Oswin breathed, breaking away from Alys's side and racing toward the great house. He pulled his sleeve over his nose and mouth as he vanished inside.

"Your Highness," Basir called after him, then looked around quickly for a less impulsive approach than merely dashing inside at his own peril. He spotted the large pond, which remained relatively untouched by the destruction that had barreled in not long before their arrival. "Robin."

The Fae turned with a ballerina's grace and extended her arms towards the fountain, her fingers curling ever so slightly to beckon the water to her. It twisted up and out like a large ribbon dancing in the breeze, her magic coaxing it to follow after her into the house and after the flames.

Basir drew his sword, gave Alys an uncomfortable look, and muttered, "Wait here," before entering the house himself.

Alys could hear a distant sizzle, which reminded her of water evaporating on the burner from a pot boiling over. She shifted back and forth from foot to foot, feeling absolutely useless. As the sizzling sound dissipated, she moved closer to the house, assuming that Robin had put out enough of the fire that it was safe to do so.

The air was still thick with smoke, and while the smell was not particularly familiar, something about the way it stung her eyes, or made it hard to see, was. Instinctively, she brought her sleeve to her nose and mouth, and, for reasons she couldn't quite explain, felt compelled to walk as quietly as she could manage.

Despite the fact that she'd been in the Duchess' home before, she found herself perplexed by the layout. It was disorienting. Her feet anticipated taking her down a small corridor that should have existed immediately to her right, but her eyes confirmed that no passage existed.

Instead she took the closest thing — the hallway that led down to the library. Her careful footfalls on the hardwood floor were uneasy. Shouldn't there have been carpet beneath her?

She closed her eyes briefly and remembered lying on green shag carpeting, running her fingers over it like it'd been grass. She remembered having to cover her nose and sneak to her room so she didn't choke on the smoke.

Alys stopped abruptly. *Her* room? She realized there was something about the smoke filled hallways that was familiar that had nothing to do with the Duchess' home at all. A place she'd been, a place she'd *lived*, a place that had once been her own but had somehow been completely forgotten. It was unsettling.

She reached out to the right wall, her hand searching for a doorknob that wasn't there. She stopped and looked at the fire blackened wall, confused before looking down at her hand. What had she been reaching for?

Alys shook her head and continued on towards the library. The great doors were partially open.

They must have been closed during the fire because, as she pulled them back just enough to slip inside, the room inside was completely untouched by flames. Without the haze of smoke, the dream of the other house she couldn't place faded from her mind.

"Rosalind?" she called out, not really expecting an answer.

The library seemed to be as they'd left it, her memory book still sitting closed on the table.

She fingered the cover and turned back a page curiously. It was completely blank. Her brow furrowed and she turned another — also blank. "Guess that makes sense," she muttered, taking a handful of pages so she could flip through them rapidly with her thumb, but the pages stuck somewhere in the middle as they hit an inconsistency, falling open to where a folded page had been tucked into the binding.

Now that certainly hadn't been there the first time she'd looked through it. It was thicker than the other pages, made of some kind of parchment paper.

Alys plucked it from the crease and looked at it. It was folded three times, and, as she opened it, she noticed that it appeared to be a copy of some kind of official document.

HER MAJESTY, THE WHITE QUEEN
OF TERRA MIRUM,
HIS HIGHNESS, THE BLACK KING
OF SHADOWS,
HER MAJESTY, THE RED QUEEN OF
THE MORNING,

DESIRING to end the state of war between FAE and DREAM, and to establish peace so that any of either people may live in serenity and security,

HAVE RESOLVED that the expansion of ARDEN will cease, and that full sovereignty over the FOREST OF THOUGHT and the TULGEY WOOD be returned to the DREAM.

Article I

1. The state of war between the Parties will be terminated, and peace will be established between them upon the exchange of the instruments of ratification of this Treaty.

2. Terra Mirum will withdraw all its armed forces from Arden's borders, Arden militia will resign from the Forest of Thought, and Terra Mirum will resume the exercise of full sovereignty over the forest.

3. Upon completion of the interim withdrawal, the parties will establish normal and friendly relations, in accordance with Article III (3).

Alys found Article II was no more than a detailed description of the border between the two kingdoms, and Article III was more than half cut off as there seemed to be a missing page that was nowhere to be found. What she did find, however, explained why Rosalind had hid it in the first place.

Article III

1. As a sign of sincerity for desiring peace between their two kingdoms, HER MAJESTY, THE RED QUEEN OF THE MORNING and HIS HIGHNESS, THE BLACK KING OF SHADOWS present a COLERIDGE CLOCK.

In honor of the great battles fought and the warriors who gave their lives, HER MAJESTY, THE QUEEN OF TERRA MIRUM presents a VORPAL BLADE.

The doors burst open and Alys startled, looking to see Oswin, Basir, Robin and Smoke all poised for a fight, only to relax sheepishly once they saw her.

"I thought I told you to wait outside," Basir grumbled.

"Did you find the duchess?" Alys asked cautiously, completely ignoring Basir's disdain.

Smoke's eyes shamefully slid to the side. "No. They took her."

"Then why burn the house?"

"Likely to smoke out any of us who might have been hiding from them when they arrived," Oswin explained. He sheathed his own blade and moved towards her. "Did you find something?"

Alys shook her head. "No, Rosalind did." She handed him the treaty.

Oswin looked at it curiously. "A copy of the treaty of Thought?"

"Read the last bit." Alys pointed down to Article III and watched as his eyes scanned over it once, and then again.

"Robin." Oswin held out the treaty to the Queen's Rhyme, pointing at the same article that Alys had indicated to him.

The Fae took the parchment carefully, eyeing both Oswin and Alys suspiciously before reading it for herself. "The vorpal blade was a peace gift?" She looked stunned.

Smoke visibly stiffened.

"So the blade not only exists, but it's no longer in the castle." Basir seemed conflicted, but turned his attention to his wife's confusion. "It would have happened prior to either of us taking our positions at court, my love."

"But why is this record not among the others?" Robin answered. "I've never actually seen this treaty anywhere in the castle records. How could I have not known this? Why...why did she keep this from me?"

"The second page is missing, so I cannot speak for the witnesses, but if I recall from my father, it was a very small and private ceremony," Basir explained. "I am sure it had nothing to do with Queen Aislynn's trust in you, my love, and everything to do with not wanting her own people to know she had given away a Royal Family heirloom, let alone a piece of our history, to the very people who started The Great War in the first place. Regardless that it was for the sake of peace, it would not have earned her any favors. She was still very young at the time—too young, I believe, was the argument circulating around the court at the time of her coronation."

Robin nodded reluctantly, seeing the reason in Basir's words, though they gave little comfort. "Which meant it was imperative to keep up appearances, especially in her first year on the throne."

"Which explains why these records would not have been kept at the palace," Oswin said. "My mother must have entrusted Rosalind with one of the only copies."

"Isn't the blade not being in the castle a good thing, though?" Alys asked. "We can get to it before confronting the Nightmare personally."

"Yes," Oswin said. "If he agrees to give it up."

"If *who* agrees?"

"Oberon." Smoke spoke the name in a hushed tone and his voice almost sounded hoarse from it. His typically cool composure was lost, and he shifted uncomfortably from side to side, suddenly restless and eager to leave the room.

"He's not *completely* unreasonable," Robin stated cautiously.

"Not completely unreasonable," Smoke snorted, looking away. "He's a tyrant who'd curse his own wife to get his way, but he's not *completely* unreasonable."

"We'll appeal to Titania, then," Oswin tried to reason.

"Wait, wait, wait...back up" Alys held up her hands. "Oberon and Titania?"

"The King and Queen of the Fae Courts," Basir said.

"As in *Shakespeare's* Oberon and Titania?"

Robin bristled and muttered something that sounded suspiciously like "bastard" under her breath.

"Oh, good, you're familiar. Less to explain." Basir wrapped an arm around Robin's shoulders.

"You're saying it's true?"

"Mostly true," Basir said carefully.

Robin cleared her throat loudly and shrugged off her husband's arm.

"Based on real events," Basir hastily corrected himself. "There were, of course, plenty of artistic embellishments and inaccuracies."

"Like what?"

"The mortal King and Queen and their relationship to the royals of the Fae court, the fleeing lovers from Athens— "

"The fact I'm not a *man*," Robin said with clear irritation that this was not mentioned first. Or perhaps it was something more. Alys noticed something flicker in Robin's eyes that she could not quite place. Regret? Whatever it was, she was clearly directing the conversation away from it as fast as she could manage. She looked at Alys. "Word of advice, kid, never anger a writer. You make an ass of them once and they make sure you pay for it for the rest of your life." She muttered the rest to herself. "Even if they do think they just dreamed it."

"So...you're *that* Robin? I mean, Puck? The hobgoblin, the—"

"I'm *Fae,* just like the rest of them," Robin snapped. "I don't have goat's feet or try to get travelers lost in the forest at night or any other horrible thing that bitter little man wrote about me. At least...I don't do that anymore. *Much*." She waves her hands dismissively, clearly flustered. "Look, he was acting like an ass, so I thought it'd be funny if he looked like one. It was a harmless prank, and it lasted barely an hour. It was just a little fun. I'm not a *monster*."

"I don't think Alys was implying you were." Basir rubbed the woman's shoulders soothingly. "Puck was Robin's name when she served the Unseelie Court at Arden."

Alys looked confused, so Robin elaborated. "There was a special unit of us who performed some of the more...*delicate* tasks. We were each given a code name."

"Why?"

"You seem fairly familiar with our Mr. Shakespeare," Smoke finally spoke up. "Has he written *Romeo and Juliet* yet? The old, 'What's in a name? That which we call a rose would smell as sweet' line?"

Alys nodded cautiously.

"Well, it's bullshit," Smoke concluded. "Here, words have power, and your name can mean everything. Here, there are certain creatures who can control the very blood in your veins just by knowing your name."

"Like the Nightmare," Oswin whispered.

"So that's why you go by Smoke?"

"That's why he *still* goes by Smoke," Robin answered delicately as if walking over eggshells. "Silas and I used to serve together under Oberon's command—but his service was not by choice."

Smoke walked past them, snatching the

treaty from Robin's hand to examine it himself over by the window.

"It's...not a fond memory for him. For either of us, to be honest…"

"Titania will listen to you," Smoke said to Oswin as if the conversation hadn't just skirted so close to traumatic memories. He turned from the window and pressed the treaty into Oswin's hand. "She was very fond of your mother, and if you remind her how Arden *will* suffer should we lose our hold on Terra Mirum, you'll have no trouble convincing her to help you."

"What do you mean help *you*?" Oswin asked.

"He means he's not coming with us," Basir answered as if he'd been anticipating this moment of abandonment since Smoke joined them.

"Ten points for the man with the dapper hat." Smoke smiled half-heartedly.

"She'd want to see you," Robin murmured. "I'm sure she misses you, and having you there will only help us."

"You don't need my help as much as Rosalind right now."

"You're going back?" Robin looked unsure.

Smoke bit his lip and rested his hands on the Fae's shoulders, his brow furrowed. "I hesitated once and it cost you your brother's life. There is nothing I can do to atone for that, not now, not ever, but I will make sure no one else pays for my mistakes. And, yes, my motives are selfish, and I realize now had Rosalind and Jack's places been reversed, I would not have been able to act so coldly in the name of strategy. I don't expect you to forgive me for that, and I will not dare ask for it. While I ensure Rosalind's safety, you will need to bargain with Oberon for more than just the sword, and I can help with that."

Robin frowned. "What are you talking about?"

"The Nightmare has taken control of too many, and our only hope of combating that is not with a weapon. We need to bring an army with us. It's the only way. They're immune to the corruption. The Nightmares will pose far less a threat to Arden and Fae if they attack now by our side."

"What makes you think Oberon will just lend us his army?" Basir asked.

Smoke smiled grimly and looked to Basir, his hands dropping from Robin's shoulders as he stood up straight. "Not lend, my friend, *rent*. We're going to convince them that an alliance against the Nightmares is in their best interest, and then we are going to purchase their services."

"With what?" Basir raised an eyebrow.

Smoke took a deep breath. "With *me*."

Chapter 15

The Road To Arden

"We're really going to let him go through with it?" They'd gone their separate ways and left Untimely Manor nearly an hour ago. They'd walked in silence before Robin voiced her concerns. The conflict had been raging inside her, a battle between necessity and empathy.

"You heard him, Robin," Basir said. "If Oberon resists the idea, it's the only way to acquire an army strong enough for us to have a chance at winning this."

"I know, but..." Robin shook her head. "Even if I insisted on blaming him for Jack's death, Basir, I would not wish this upon him. I would not wish this on *anyone*. He fought so hard to leave that life, can we really just condemn him back to it? And in this manner? What he's volunteering is enslavement."

"He's always done whatever he feels needs to be done, and, unfortunately, for once I can agree with him on this. We need leverage."

"Why is Smoke leverage?" Alys finally piped up, no longer able to contain her growing curiosity about the situation.

Robin looked over her shoulder as they climbed around and over the great roots in this part of the forest. As the only one of the party who'd ever made the trek from Terra Mirum to Arden, she'd taken the lead. "Smoke is half-human."

Alys's eyes widened, but, despite her surprise at this news, she wasn't entirely sure what to make of it. "I don't understand."

"There are some humans that have a certain kind of power in our world, Dreamers, I believe is what Smoke called them — it's the same reason you dream of here or The Nothing. No one is sure why we're so connected. We just always have been. We *do* know that should one of these humans ever physically tread in our world, that same connection gives them the power to actually alter our world," Oswin explained.

"*I* have that power?" Alys's jaw dropped.

Basir made a hissing sound by sucking in a breath through his gritted teeth.

Robin rested a hand on Basir's arm as they walked. "Yes, but, much like dreaming, it's completely unreliable, and, for obvious reasons, should not be attempted."

"What obvious reasons?" Alys asked. "If I can get rid of this Nightmare myself, right now, just tell me how to do it."

"Because, more likely than not, you'd get rid of all of us." Basir's normally calm demeanor seemed strained, almost panicked. "Or The Nothing altogether, and then Nightmares would overrun Terra Mirum as other humans continued to create them while they sleep. Like we said, it's complicated and extremely unreliable, and *should not be attempted.*"

"Being only half-human, Smoke can change himself, but not the fabric of anything around him, which makes him a valuable asset, but not a danger to Dreams or Terra Mirum," Robin explained.

Alys half-remembered Smoke telling her to shrink. She recalled him convincing her that consuming a mushroom would cause her to change size, and the flower that had returned her to normal. Had she really done that on her own? Had it not been the flower at all?

"He's also half Fae." Robin's continued explanation broke Alys' train of thought. "His mother was one of Titania's court, and his father was a poet from your world."

"Another one of Shakespeare's exploits?" Alys asked with a half-smile. She was starting to notice the trees were getting harder and harder to maneuver around, but, at this point, she wasn't sure if it was because the trees were getting bigger or if, somehow, they were getting smaller.

"No." Robin snorted. "Though I think he did write something about it in that *quaint* little play of his."

Alys had never heard the word "quaint" sound so hostile, and she and Oswin exchanged an amused glance.

"No, his name was Coleridge. You don't by chance happen to know him too, do you?"

"Samuel Taylor Coleridge?" Alys looked back at Oswin, who looked straight ahead and pretended not to notice her.

"Huh, guess he's famous when you're from, too." Robin seemed impressed.

"*When* I'm from?"

"Time works on a linear plane in your world," Basir explained. "Here it's...well, it's different, that's for sure —"

"Simply put, Fae have the ability to travel to any point they choose on your timeline. Coleridge was born after Shakespeare on your world, but met Ila and fathered Silas before we all met Shakespeare. Make sense?"

Alys ducked too late under a branch and hit her head. "I guess?" She rubbed the sore spot and looked back, realizing she'd ducked down under an oversized root and not a branch at all. She craned her head back and looked up at the enormous trunk of the tree that stretched high and out of view. Even the plants that grew around the trees were larger than life. "Coleridge wouldn't have anything to do with a Coleridge clock, would he?"

Basir looked to Oswin, who was still pretending he was oblivious to the conversation, and asked. "Where did you hear about that?"

"It was in the treaty." Alys shrugged and Oswin finally looked at her, a little surprised she hadn't mentioned him showing her his pocket watch. "Terra Mirum gave Arden the vorpal blade. Arden gave Terra Mirum something called the Coleridge Clock. What does it do exactly?"

Oswin mouthed *Thank you.*

"Ah. Well…" Basir looked to Robin as if trying to decide if this was information meant to be shared, but Robin seemed to be trying to decide that same thing for herself. It wasn't the sort of thing you wanted an unwanted Dreamer to really know about. "It um…"

Oswin decided for both of them. "It's a device that allows someone without magic to travel from your world to ours. Ila created it so her lover could meet her in Arden."

Alys tilted her head slightly towards the pocket where she'd seen Oswin carry his watch.

"And I used it to escape the Nightmare into your world," Oswin explained.

"Oberon stole it after Ila died in childbirth to prevent anyone from using it," Robin explained.

"People can still die in childbirth here? But you have *magic*. Doesn't that kind of fix everything. Like magic?"

"Changeling births aren't safe, Alys." Robin almost sounded like she was issuing some kind of warning. "I don't think Coleridge ever really found out. I think he suspected that Shakespeare's changeling boy may have been about Silas and Ila, but he had no way of getting back to Arden once Oberon found out about them. Can't imagine what losing your family like that would do to a person."

Alys nodded thoughtfully and fell silent, mulling the thought over in her head. It was harder to imagine than she would have thought. Not because the idea of losing a loved one was so foreign, but the disturbing realization that she couldn't remember her family. Surely she must have had one.

Oswin nudged her with his elbow. "Are you feeling all right?"

Alys forced a smile and nodded awkwardly. "Y-yeah...I was just...thinking about Coleridge." It wasn't entirely a lie, and so it seemed excusable. "They say he suffered from crippling bouts of depression and an opium addiction throughout his adult life. Diagnosed as bipolar disorder, but now I wonder if it was because of this."

Oswin's expression was a mixture of sorrow and intrigue. "You seem to know a lot about these poets and their work."

"There isn't exactly a lot to do where I grew up in Appleweed. When I wasn't with Charlie, I read."

"You and Charlie are good friends?"

"The best of friends," Alys answered with a smile that almost instantly clouded over as an unexplained ache split through her core.

"Something wrong?"

"No...well..." Alys hesitated and dropped her voice even lower. "Is it possible my memory book didn't have everything in it?"

Oswin frowned. "Can you not remember something?"

"A few things, but, almost more than that, I feel like I've forgotten something very important."

He reached out his hand and wiggled his fingers a little, and Alys took his hand, her fingers wagging between his before fully intertwining. "We'll talk to Smoke when this is all over," he promised.

Alys gave his hand a squeeze. "Okay."

Oswin looked down at their hands. "Are you cold?"

"I'm always cold," she answered with a wry smile. "That's what happens when you're born in Appleweed. The cold seeps in and never leaves."

"Sounds like a great place for a holiday," he remarked facetiously.

"I know, right?" Alys laughed a little and let their hands swing between them. "Charlie used to say that it's not the end of the world, but you can see it from there."

Oswin chuckled. "I imagine that's why you left, then?"

"No, I..." Alys's smile faded again as the ache hit her again. "I can't remember why I left..."

"At all?"

Alys felt her eyes stinging again and she wiped at them with her free hand as she shook her head. "I remember the diner and MaryAnn and Charlie— "

"MaryAnn?" he asked, remembering the name Alys had given him upon their first meeting.

"She and I worked together at her mother's restaurant." She squirmed sheepishly when she caught Oswin's expression. "Don't look at me like that. You could have been a crazy stalker or something. I'm not going to tell a crazy stalker my real name."

"Because not knowing your real name is going to prevent a maniac from killing you in a train tunnel." Oswin gave her a look.

Alys stopped, realizing she hadn't considered this. "Well, anything sounds stupid when you say it like that," she defended herself half-heartedly.

"I grew up in Elan Vital," Oswin offered, letting their arms swing together now. "It was the epicenter of culture, then. Everything you ever wanted to see, everything you ever wanted to learn—it was right at your fingertips. The absolute heart of Terra Mirum, Alys, with theater and lectures and the best food you've ever tasted."

"So you grew up in the exact *opposite* of Appleweed," Alys pointed out.

Oswin laughed. "I suppose so…" His face fell and he exhaled slowly, shaking his head. "My mother made it the most beautiful place you've ever seen. I can't believe what *that thing* has done to it..."

Alys tugged his hand, forcing him to stumble a little into her and their shoulders to bump. "What was she like, your mother?"

He smiled briefly. "Kind—above all. She was a compassionate ruler, and ridiculously clever. Her strategies are what ended The Great War with the Fae, you know."

Alys smiled. "Really?"

Oswin nodded fondly. "I don't intend to speak ill of my father when I say this—he's a good man, and a great king--but I don't think Terra Mirum would have been the same without my mother." He chewed his lower lip. "I don't think it *will* be the same without her."

"It will have you."

"Yeah," Oswin agreed grimly, a bitterness creeping into his demeanor. "And look at the great good, I've done."

Alys looked at him thoughtfully, wondering if there was a way she could quite literally push the weight off his shoulders. "Earlier, back at Rosalind's, you said the Nightmare could control people just by knowing their name. You knew that because she'd already done it to you once before, hadn't she?" Alys's eyes softened. "That's why you were having so much trouble back at the garden. Whatever she did to you—you were trying to fight it off again."

"The night she came to the palace, I didn't even know anything was wrong until the guards woke me." He bowed his head, and his eyes focused on their feet. "That thing murdered my mother while we slept, and I was completely oblivious."

Something in his words really resonated with Alys. His tone, that absolute frustration with himself, almost seemed familiar. She found herself empathizing, feeling a mixture of anger and humiliation for sleeping while Charlie...while Charlie *what*?

"I wish I could have done more for her, more for Robin and Jack," Oswin admitted. "I know wishing is useless. But you have to understand, Alys, she gets in you—her voice. You've heard beats that you can't help moving to, right?"

Alys nodded.

"Her voice gets in you like that and it just... it burrows into your heart until it's beating in that same damned rhythm, and, before you know it, you don't even have control over your own limbs. And the worst part is, *you know* you don't have control, but you can't even scream for help because you don't own your own voice anymore. And all you can do to fight it is to do everything you can to keep your heartbeat on its own rhythm. It's... maddening."

"I'm sorry."

Oswin didn't answer, and, as the silence fell between them, despite their still interlocked fingers, Alys felt him growing distant.

Alys called ahead to the other two who had gained quite a bit of a lead on them. "Hey Robin, did you really turn Shakespeare into a donkey?"

Oswin breathed a small laugh beside her and nudged her shoulder with his own, assuring her that, for the moment, she'd kept him with them.

Robin herself didn't answer directly, but Alys almost swore she could hear the smile in her voice. "We're getting close to the perimeter. We should try to be quiet so we don't alarm—"

"Any guards waiting for you?" A voice finished for her as a Fae armed to the very teeth swung out from behind one of the impossibly large roots. Despite her trappings of war, she seemed friendly enough since she promptly hugged Robin so tightly Alys was worried she might burst. "Aw, Puck, you've gotten sloppy! I knew you were coming for a mile, at least. Been in court too long. It's made you soft.

"Good to see you too, Moth." She pried herself away, falling into Basir in the process.

"This would be the husband, then?" Moth studied the tall man with a critical eye. "Bit stuffier than I would have imagined, I have to admit."

Basir was about to retort, but not before his wife offered, "You'd be surprised how much changes behind closed doors," which caused his mouth to simply hang open uselessly, having lost all words.

Robin didn't give him time to find them as she gestured to the blades and bow that hung every which way on the other Fae. "Expecting something else?"

Moth shrugged. "Not really, but the Queen seems convinced *something* is coming our way, so we don't want to be unprepared. What brings you back here?" Her nearly black eyes shifted to Oswin and Alys as they approached. "With royalty in tow, no less."

Oswin frowned. "The something coming your way."

Moth looked from the prince to Robin, who only gave a grim sort of nod. She turned her head upwards and called, "Cobweb, I need to leave my post. Send someone on ahead to tell the Queen." Her only answer was a soft rustle high above them, but it must have meant something, because she turned her attention back to the party. "Come with me."

Chapter 16

THE RED COURT

Arden was almost entirely surrounded by the great trees they'd climbed over and through in order to reach it. They formed a protective kind of wall around the kingdom that had undoubtedly created a certain advantage during the war between Fae and Dream.

Alys found herself craning her neck back to look up as Moth led them towards the castle, trying desperately to see where the tops of the trees might be. She vaguely wondered if the reason everyone believed fairies were small was because, seen next to these trees, she didn't look much taller than a chipmunk herself.

She noticed these trees were not only different from the rest of the forest in size, but in general appearance, as well. These looked more like weeping willows, the branches reaching out and intertwining with other trees while the leaves draped down towards their heads as if beckoning to be climbed.

Some kind of lights had been strung down the branches, giving the illusion that fireflies had been caught in the thick, leafy curtains during their travels across the night sky. Homes had been built up along the tall trunks, and some had even been hollowed out into rooms and glass placed in knots to make windows, the light inside creating a soft glow that emanated through the wood and peeked through the ridges in the bark.

If stars grew on trees, Alys imagined it would have looked something like this. She tugged on Oswin's sleeve and pointed upward.

His mouth parted a little, his jaw dropping ever so slightly in awe as the two of them nearly stumbled down the path with their gazes fixed high above them.

Alys looked down in time to see two fairies standing off the footpath laughing and exchanging a look she'd often seen locals give over enthusiastic tourists when she visited Seattle.

Seattle. She'd been going to Seattle to see Brian. She was going to tell him...tell him...

"I've read about this city," Oswin confessed. "And my mother spoke of it fondly, but never in all my reading could I have imagined this."

"*I* could," Alys answered, trying to sound cool. "But I'm a Dreamer. Imagination is kinda my thing."

Oswin poked her in the ribs.

Alys's laughter alerted Basir, who looked back with an expression that could only be defined as scolding.

Oswin cleared his throat and shoved his hands in his pockets, directing his attention to the trees to his side.

Alys raised her eyebrows and looked between the two men as Basir stared ahead again and began talking quietly to Robin.

"So..." Oswin started in a low voice, trying to look like his attention was still fixed on the scenery. "She-Who-Reads-A-Lot—"

"That should be my Indian name," Alys observed wryly.

"Your what?" He turned a very confused expression toward her and all pretense of being more interested in their surroundings than her was lost.

"Never mind. Bad human joke. Kind of offensive. *Really* offensive, actually. In fact, now that I've had time to think about it, I'm very glad you didn't get it. Appleweed is… stupid things rub off on you and…please say something so I shut up and stop making an absolute idiot of myself."

Oswin shook his head with a bewildered laugh and continued with his original line of thought. "What do you know about the Fae?"

"I know…" Alys trailed off, looking around them. "They have wings, live in trees, and some of them are named Robin and Moth."

"So you know nothing."

"Those were things."

"So you know nothing *useful*."

"Don't be an asshole."

Oswin stopped, and, for a moment, they just stared at each other until they both turned simultaneously forward, each unsure if they might have actually offended the other.

"I've never talked with someone like this before," he admitted. Even though Alys wasn't looking at him, she could hear a smile in his voice.

"I haven't talked with someone like this since Charlie." Alys paused. Since?

"It's...nice."

"Yeah..."

"You called me an asshole," he laughed, shaking his head.

"You were *being* an asshole."

"I don't think anyone has ever called me that in all my life."

"Maybe not to your face," Alys said under her breath.

Oswin opened his mouth to retort but couldn't think of anything clever to say. He huffed a little, pretending to be indignant, and failed miserably at hiding the growing smile on his face.

Alys put her own hands in her sweatshirt pockets and used her elbow to nudge his. "Tell me about fairies."

"Fine, fine, fine." Oswin looked up above them, collecting his thoughts. "Well, the first thing you should know is that there are two courts, the Seelie and the Unseelie, the light and the dark, or the red and the black courts."

"Red?"

"It's the color of life."

"So...what? There's life and death, good and evil?"

Oswin shook his head. "No, it's not that black and white."

"Because it's black and *red*," Alys asserted with an impish grin.

"Are you going to let me explain this or not?"

Alys smiled, pretended to zip her mouth, and gestured for him to proceed.

"Back in the day, the Seelie did tend to favor order and help humans, while the Unseelie leaned towards misleading them and dabbled in chaos, but, mostly they both controlled the cycle of the seasons. Consequently, their occasional presence on earth accidentally started a lot of religions — or, in some cases, not so accidentally."

Alys tilted her head a little curiously at him.

"For about a century, Oberon thought the idea of humans mistaking him for a god was the funniest thing in all the realms. From what I understand, it caused a lot of problems. A *lot* of problems."

"Huh," said Alys. "Well, that puts all of our religious contentions and piety into a very interesting light."

"Mm." Oswin gave a strained smile. "Anyway, the nobility of the two courts married in an effort to keep the world in balance."

"Titania and Oberon."

Oswin tapped the side of his nose with his finger. "Exactly. And, for the most part, the arrangement has worked, but every now and then there's a fight and all hell breaks loose, the elements fall out of alignment, and the world goes a little upside down."

"Therefore the winds, piping to us in vain, as in revenge, have sucked up from the sea contagious fogs, which falling in the land, have every pelting river made so proud, that they have overborne their continents," Alys recited quietly, shaking her head in amusement at the reality of one of her favorite plays taking shape around them.

Oswin looked sidelong at her and just smiled. "Exactly..."

"Lot of pressure on a marriage," Alys pointed out.

Moth led them up a set of stairs that had been carved into one of the roots of the tree that was more or less in the center in the city. It brought them to a door which had been carved intricately with depictions and symbols of the four seasons.

It was almost too much detail and design. Alys felt afraid to touch anything, and as the set of doors opened to the throne room, this theme only continued.

A floral scent greeted them, the room filled with a strange red flower that hung from pots and tall vases that lined the carpeted aisle leading up to the dais. The bloom looked familiar, but she couldn't remember what it was called.

On one side of the aisle, the room was filled with Seelie, glowing and bright as life itself. The other side, where Alys imagined the Unseelie held court, was empty, as was one of the thrones on the dais.

On the occupied throne sat a woman adorned in gold, soft red ringlets looping around the spires of her golden crown, creating a mane of fire around her pale face. Amber eyes watched their approach with a calculating stillness.

Alys thought she looked like the sun itself.

As they came to a stop, the Queen shifted her gaze to Moth and gave the minutest of nods.

Moth bowed low to the throne and turned to stand at the base of the dais, addressing them as if they hadn't just spent the past ten minutes walking together. "Her Majesty, Titania, The Red Queen of the Morning, accepts your audience. State your name and business."

It wasn't until Moth and Robin were standing next to an entire flock of Seelie that it occurred to her that they weren't one of them. By comparison, they almost seemed muted—especially Moth, who, unlike Robin, still wore the dark armor of the Unseelie. The Seelie themselves were adorned in vibrantly colored fabric, but even more than that their skin, while no particular shade among them, seemed to glow.

"Your Majesty," Robin addressed the queen respectfully and bowed, presenting Oswin. "His Highness, Oswin, The White Prince of Terra Mirum."

Somehow, Alys had forgotten Oswin was royalty, and hearing his title announced so formally made her palms clammy.

Titania raised her hand, her fingers long and slender like the stem of the flower that was so celebrated in her decorations. "In this case, I feel introductions seem superfluous." Her voice was as clear as a summer day. She smiled warmly. "You're Aislynn's boy. I've known you since you were but a little rabbit of a thing. Always scurrying about, late for studies. I hope that punctuality has improved."

"As do I, Your Majesty," Oswin returned.

"How is your mother?"

Alys watched the way Oswin's throat constricted as he swallowed as if trying to keep down a meal. "Dead." He scarcely spoke above a whisper, yet it seemed to resonate in the hall and cause the Seelie, even Titania, to sharply intake a breath. "*Murdered.*"

The Seelie erupted into a cacophony of whispers that were silenced as abruptly as they had started when Titania raised her hand once more. She leaned forward in her throne. "Murdered?" Disbelief danced along the melody of her voice. "By whom?"

"A Nightmare, Your Majesty. A Nightmare escaped from The Nothing itself."

Again the whispers started, quieter this time. Titania looked as if she'd been struck. "Moth," she said quietly. "Fetch my lord. I'm afraid this matter demands his immediate attention."

Moth moved past them as quickly as she could manage without knocking anyone over.

"When?" The Red Queen demanded of the group.

"But two days ago, three perhaps?" Oswin answered. "It has not been an easy journey, I'm afraid it's all blending together."

"Oh, my sweet sister," Titania breathed, a hand to her mouth as she sat back in the throne. "How could this happen?"

"We aren't exactly sure, Your Majesty," Robin spoke up. "The guards were missing from their post at The Door, and our guards were acting under her orders by the time most of us awoke. The Nightmare took the castle completely by surprise."

"So she had help from someone," a deep voice said from the back of the court.

"His Royal Highness, Oberon, the Black King of Shadows," Moth announced from the back.

Oberon moved with an almost militant precision, many of the Unseelie sweeping into their place in court behind him like a murder of crows. Much like Oswin had previously described, there was nothing evil about them, per se, but they did seem to carry the darker things about the world with them. So much so that light itself seemed to shine a little dimmer in their presence.

Alys noticed that as Oberon swept past them and up the aisle that the row of flowers closest to him lost their petals and died as if passing through their life cycle at an accelerated pace.

Where his wife seemed aflame like the summer heat, he was the epitome of winter, even leaving frostbitten footprints on the ground, which melted almost immediately after he took another step. He took Titania by the hand and brushed his lips over her knuckles before taking his own throne and regarding the small group like a bird of prey. "And you've come here because you think it was one of us." He looked to Robin, whose head was bowed more out of habit than anything else. "Oh, and you've even brought my own in in order to accuse us."

"No, Your Highness, we have not come to insult your house by laying accusations at your feet. We came for the vorpal blade." Oswin spoke with a level, almost regal, tone in the face of the accusation, but Alys noticed his knuckles tightening behind his back as a means of maintaining his composure. He was nervous. They were *all* nervous in this man's presence.

"The vorpal blade..." Oberon repeated. "You've come to reclaim the very item that your mother presented to us as a sign of your everlasting friendship? The prize of my armory?"

"We've come to ask for the only known weapon capable of slaying a Nightmare," Oswin clarified.

"Ah," Oberon mused. "Convenient. And what sort of prize should I receive in return, should I give you my greatest treasure?"

"The changeling has offered to return to your ranks in exchange for the sword and your aid," Robin spoke softly.

Oberon became very still. "You're lying," he said doubtfully.

"By the night, I speak the truth," Robin answered.

The King snapped his fingers and Robin looked up seemingly involuntarily, and, for a moment, they stared at each other. Alys wondered if he was quite literally searching her mind for her sincerity. When he looked away, he shifted in his seat, clearly enticed by this offer. "Why would he do this?"

"He believes Terra Mirum's freedom is worth the price of his own," Robin answered.

"If we do not have the sword, we cannot hope to win against this creature," Oswin asserted. "Nor can we do it without the help of an army."

"An army?" Oberon echoed, his attention sharpening once more. "First you beg for my most prized possession, and now you expect the aid of my army. How much do you need, I wonder, to conquer but one Nightmare?"

"This Nightmare possesses great power, including the ability to turn men against their own will. She's already captured all of Elan Vital. Not one citizen remains free from her control."

"A Jabberwock?" Titania asked in a hushed tone.

"No." Oswin shook his head. "We don't believe so, but it is quite certain she is a Horror of some kind."

The room murmured uncomfortably.

Oberon placed a hand over Titania's comfortingly. "For what reason would I send my own people against a Horror? One soldier, regardless of how valuable an asset he may be, is not worth the price of both the blade and my militia."

"What about your *treaty*?" Alys blurted out.

Absolute silence followed, and everyone slowly turned to look at her.

Oberon slowly came to a stand and fixed his eyes on the dark-haired girl, really looking at her for the first time. He fixed a cold gaze on her like a hawk regarding its next chosen meal. "Do my eyes deceive me, Your Highness, or is there a mortal among your ranks?"

Alys met his gaze without reservation, much to the shock and disapproval of both the Seelie and Unseelie around her.

"You see correctly." Oswin tried to keep both his voice and expression stoic. He knew the full weight of her offense, and despite her breach of protocol, he couldn't help but admire the absolute fearlessness it required. "This is Alys of Earth. She's a Dreamer."

"Interesting..." Oberon murmured, something shifting in his demeanor as he peered at her. "Then I will forgive your lack of manners this once on account of your obvious ignorance. The Treaty of Thought is a cease-fire only, ending hostile interactions between our kingdoms. Had you studied it fully, you would know that. We are bound to remain peaceful in our relations to Terra Mirum, but hold no obligation to aiding it from other threats." He moved to sit again.

"Clever loophole," Alys commented. Oswin's eyes widened and Basir's face looked like he'd been slapped full force.

Oberon stopped and turned slowly to face her again. "What did you say to me, *mortal*?"

Alys was unblinking, her chin lifting ever so slightly as she met the King of Shadows' gaze once more. "You may make no attacks on Terra Mirum, but say if something else did and then wiped out the Dream Kingdom, you would then be free to attack that hostile entity without breaking your treaty." Alys shrugged. "And why wouldn't you? It just decimated your allies, so what's to stop it from attacking you, as well? It would be self-defense. No one could blame you for self-defense, not for defending your people. And, luckily for you, you conveniently hold the only weapon that can stop it."

No one breathed.

Titania looked to Oberon. While she could not bring herself to believe the accusation, she could not deny it was out of his abilities. "Husband?"

Oberon exhaled slowly. "By the stars, you *are* a Dreamer. And what a story you have imagined for me." He sat down, unsettled by the defiance of the human girl before him. "But I assure you, it is just a story." He gestured to Moth. "They may go."

Alys pushed past the Unseelie who tried to usher her outside. "Even so, they *will* come for you. Nightmares consume all they can, and what they cannot consume, they will destroy. Once Terra Mirum falls, do you think she will be satisfied? Do you think you will be safe simply because you are saved for last? You are not immune to her magic. She's *already* taken one of your own."

Oberon held up his hand, stopping Moth from reaching for Alys again. "Who of our own?"

"My brother..." Robin spoke, and, for the first time, Alys could see the strain of not having the time to mourn weighing on her.

"Jack?" The Shadow King's face softened. The anger and arrogance melted into an emotion Alys had thought him completely incapable of—sorrow.

"His eyes were so hollow... I don't know what she did to him, or how, but I think he was dead even before his public execution." Robin's voice was tight, and she met no one's eyes in an attempt to keep the tears gathering in her own at bay. "My baby brother, who may have not been the cleverest of Fae, nor the strongest, but was loyal and good. And he loved Arden more than anything. He was taken from Thought. He'd been looking for clues next to The Nothing in order to free Arden of any blame for this ordeal, and to locate the real traitor. The Nightmare beheaded him for treason as an example to any who would oppose her."

Basir set his hands on her shoulders.

Robin layered one hand over his while the other covered her nose and mouth to suppress a sob as the tears won out.

Alys swallowed hard and looked from Robin to the thrones. "She has Terra Mirum's army, and, even under its late Queen, you admitted defeat. What kind of terrible force do you think they'll be with a Horror driving them forward?"

Titania looked to Oberon, who stood once more, this time having far more trouble staying steady on his feet. "Very well, Alys of Earth, you have your army. We will help you."

Chapter 17

ONCE MORE UNTO THE BREACH

"We'll have the cover of night," Moth observed, indicating the absolute blackness that loomed above them as she helped equip Robin with her old weapons. "No moon."

"Hopefully, that will work with us and not against us," Basir observed, weighing both possibilities in his mind. "It will grant us stealth, but also give the Nightmare strength."

Oswin joined them, a sword at his hip and another sheathed in a scabbard in his hands. "That's the optimistic spirit, Basir," he said with a grim smile. "Can always count on you to keep up morale."

"The darkness *will* be to her advantage. Nightmares are naturally strengthened by the shadows. We can't discount that. Our only hope for victory lies in strategy. I'm only trying to look at this battle with a critical eye, Your Highness," Basir said. "We must approach this logically."

"As has been your profession since long before my birth," Oswin noted with a smile.

"You're rather cheerful for someone on the brink of war," Alys observed.

"Well, someone has to keep up spirits." Oswin shook his head and turned to face her. "Plus, I'm fairly certain nothing has entirely sunk in yet. I still can't believe you talked to Oberon like that."

"Are you upset?"

"No, we wouldn't be where we are if you hadn't spoken up. Though, I must say, while I have more questions than answers, I'm relieved it wasn't our allies who let the Nightmare free."

"Alys's big mouth saves the day," she mused. "Who knew?"

"He could have struck you down, turned you into something horrible, and yet you didn't even flinch." He looked at her in absolute wonder. "It's like you weren't even the slightest bit scared of what might happen."

"I wasn't, really," Alys admitted confidently.

"Does nothing frighten you?"

Alys thought a moment, searching her memories for the last time she could even remember what fear felt like. She felt adrenaline, excitement, curiosity...but not fear. It was as if all of those pages had been ripped from her memory and replaced. She shook her head with a helpless smile and shrug. "Not that I know of."

"Everyone's afraid of something," Oswin said, though there was a genuine sincerity to her voice that made him doubt the truth of that statement.

Alys considered this and asked, "What do you think the Nightmare's afraid of?"

"You, if she's got any sense," Oswin laughed. He shook his head, took a deep breath, and held out the other sword to her. "Here. You should be the one to carry it."

"This is..."

"The vorpal blade. Legend says they can only be wielded by a soul who is without fear.

Honestly, I can't think of anyone more suited to that description than you after everything we've been through."

Alys caught Basir's disapproving gaze leveled on her from a short distance from behind Oswin. Her eyes shifted back to the prince and she shook her head. "I don't know if it would be right…it's your Kingdom, your heritage. *You* should be the one to carry it."

Oswin looks at her, his brow furrowed. "I could never have fathomed the reason behind our meeting in that train tunnel…but now there's not a doubt in my mind. You were drawn here to help us. Part of me wonders if my mother didn't have some hand in your arrival. Like she's still leading and helping us even now." He nodded to the blade. "Please take it. I want you to be the one."

Alys took it carefully and unsheathed it enough to look at the blade. The motion came naturally, as if she'd done it many times before. It was a familiar weight in her hands and she cradled the hilt in her right palm like she was shaking the hand of an old friend.

She could see her own face reflected back at her clearly in the blade as if it had been constructed from mirror. It projected a soft, comforting glow that cast faint shadows across her face. It reminded her of a night-light. She uncurled her fingers from the hilt so she could admire the silver grip and the odd stone that made up the pommel, which seemed to contain an ever-shifting darkness that resembled the turbulent black of The Nothing.

"What do you think?" Oswin asked.

"Simple, though the design, I have never seen its equal," Alys answered in admiration, sheathing it so she could secure the belt around her hips. "It would rival Excalibur." She stopped mid-buckle, perplexed by her own words, and blinked. Why had she said that?

"I'll be staying close to you during the battle," Oswin explained.

"Worried I can't handle it on my own?" Alys asked with a smile. Though, if she were being completely honest, she wasn't entirely sure why she was so confident that she could.

"I'm not worried about you at all," Oswin laughed, looking back towards the castle. "Not after that. I have little doubt there's anything you can't do." He slipped his hands in his pockets again. "I'm doing it for me. I think it will help if I stay close to the sword."

"I don't understand. Do you think I'm going to break it? I assure you, I'm very well trained, and I've handled far more delicate blades." Alys paused again, confused by her own words and confidence. *Had* she handled other blades? She thought a moment, and, sure enough, stumbled upon memories of other swords she had handled. They came in different designs and none handled quite the same in battle. Most notably, in her memories they had somehow seemed smaller--or had her hands been bigger?

Again, Oswin shook his head. "Due to its abilities, I think if I stay close, I'll be less likely to...I'm worried about what might happen if I encounter that voice again. I don't want to lose control."

"Oh, I see." Alys nodded in understanding. "And you think the energy from the vorpal blade may act as a kind of shield against The Nightmare's magic."

"Precisely." He turned and watched Basir and Robin as they exchanged their own private words before the battle as the rest of the army readied itself around them. Even the Seelie, who were pacifists by nature, had taken up the arms and armor to stand against what lay ahead. "I don't know what would happen if she manages to take hold of me again. What if she tells me to harm one of you?"

Alys set a hand on his shoulder comfortingly, adopting a serious tone. "Then I suppose you'll have to tell it off."

Oswin laughed in surprise. "I suppose so…" It was a brief moment of mirth before the reality of the situation loomed over her again. "I have a favor I need to ask of you."

"Beyond saving your kingdom?" Alys' mischievous smile faded as she met his gaze, realizing this was perhaps not the time to try to lighten the mood. "What is it?"

"If she takes me—"

"She won't—"

"*If she takes me*," Oswin insisted, his voice dropping to a low growl as he took a step closer to her. "I need you to…I need you to take care of me."

"What do you mean 'take care' of you?" Alys asked.

Oswin leveled his gaze with her but said nothing.

"You can't be serious."

"Basir and Robin have known me since I was a boy, they would never be able to bring themselves to do it."

"What makes you think *I* would be able to do it?" Alys demands.

"Because I'm asking you," Oswin said, resting his hands on her shoulders. "Because I *need* you to do this for me. Because I will not be a tool used to destroy the very Kingdom my own parents fought so hard to save, and because I would rather die by your hand than live as her puppet." His eyes softened and he took her hand in his. "Please, Alys. *Promise* you'll do this for me."

Alys took a deep breath, about to protest his request again, but there was something in his eyes that made her stop. *This* was what he truly wanted. She deflated, exhaling heavily. "I...I promise."

Oswin released her hand, relief overcoming him. "Thank you."

Silence fell between them, Oswin

pondering the possibility of losing himself to the Nightmare, and Alys considering the consequence of respecting his wishes.

He studied the way her brow furrowed and reached into his pocket, producing the golden watch she'd so admired before. "Here." He took her hand again, placing the watch in her palm and closed her fingers around it. "Take this with you. For luck."

Alys looked from the watch to him, and back again. "Oswin…"

"I know you're fond of arguing, but I'm not going to be moved on this either."

"It was your mother's."

"And if something happens to me, I want to make sure it's in safe hands," Oswin insisted.

"*Nothing* is going to happen to you."

"Humor me," Oswin asked. "We don't know what lies ahead."

Alys nodded and held the watch to her. "I'll keep it safe."

"May it do the same for you."

Her lips pursed. "You're irrationally stubborn. You know that, don't you?"

Oswin gave her a little half-smile. "Possibly as stubborn as you," he mused.

Alys laughed and opened her hand to look at the watch again. Her eyes widen in recognition as they trace over the etched floral design that now had a much clearer meaning to her. "I just realized, this flower..."

"It's the symbol of Titania's court," Oswin said, finally answering the question she'd asked about it upon their first meeting. "It's the proof Coleridge first took back with him to your world. It seemed an appropriate decoration for the device they used to meet in secret."

"A strange and beautiful flower." She smiled in realization, but it faded as she looked up to his face again. Her free hand absently patted her pockets and she gave a helpless shrug. "I wish I had something to give you."

"I have you," Oswin assured her, taking the Coleridge clock by the chain so he could put it over her head and hang it around her neck. "Just stay alive and that will be enough luck for me."

Alys fingered the clock idly, feeling, for the first time since she could remember, what she could only describe as nervousness. "Oswin..."

"We're moving out!" Oberon called to the battalion.

***

The Seelie's magic allowed them to make their approach on Elan Vital both fast and silent. Alys wasn't sure if the spell also impaired their own hearing or if the complete lack of noise around them was a world paralyzed into stillness. No crickets, no frogs, nor any melody typical to the evening.

Night and silence.

Then they breached the city walls and there they were.

From soldier to civilian, they were standing in a line that stretched and filled every street leading to the castle. The citizens of Elan Vital, under the Nightmare's influence, were squared against them as a human barrier. Every face seemed to look through them, like lifeless puppets that had yet to be moved into action.

"She knew we were coming," Oswin observed grimly.

"How could she not?" Robin answered.

Oswin called to those around him: "These are innocent people that this Monster means to use against us. The Nightmare's magic has them under a powerful spell, manipulating their will to her own. They know not what they do."

"Immobilize, but do not harm them if you can avoid doing so," Oberon bellowed. "Above all, seek out the Nightmare. Tonight we have her head!"

The silence spell shattered as hundreds of voices shouted in agreement and charged the line of Dreams.

Alys felt her legs carry her forward, an instinct born on what could only have been muscle memory, though what memory she wasn't even sure of as she drew the blade from its sheath at her hip. It glowed brighter as she approached, and, as she broke through the front line of her own ranks, she swung outward.

Energy crackled down the blade from the pommel, and, with the sword's sweep, she watched the group closest to her step back, leaving shadows in their place that the sword cut through like smoke. The shadows cried out and vanished into the stone on the pommel as if blown there by a great wind.

Alys was awed by the weapon in her hand and looked to the stunned people not ten feet from her who appeared to have regained their faculties. "What the...?"

"The vorpal blade is forged from the defeat of a Nightmare," Oswin explained, fending off one of his own guards. "Perhaps it can *only* kill Nightmares as a result?" The guard's blade locked with Oswin's, the prince fighting to keep his balance. "Little help?"

Alys slid her sword between Oswin's and the guard's. She turned her wrist in a circular disarm to force the sword to the guard's side. She shifted her hold on the blade and rammed the pommel into the guard's stomach. He fell backwards, but the shadow was sucked into the pommel of the sword.

Oswin almost laughed in relief and clapped Alys on the shoulders "I knew it would be smart sticking next to you. Come, we need to find The Nightmare."

The blade acted as their talisman as they moved through the crowd. On occasion, the blade passed through a body, but when Alys withdrew it, the host remained unharmed, but the shadow vanished, writhing in agony.

Alys felt as if something else guided her hand as it swung around her, Oswin at her back to keep the Dreams at bay.

The Possessed had a nightmarish quality about them as well, and she was vaguely reminded of the zombie films she and Charlie would stay up watching late at night. Their eyes were lifeless and they advanced with the kind of violent intent one was only capable when they held no personal regard for their own life. Most had weapons, but those who didn't reached out with claw-like hands, trying to snatch necks or merely slow down limbs so those who were armed had nothing to stop their attacks.

None were a match for the vorpal blade.

Alys couldn't help but feel something akin to invincible as they fought their way into the center garden. She felt like a god on the battlefield. If only Arthur could see her now—wait, what? The thought brought a pause long enough to give one of the Possessed a moment to leap upon her. She took a step back and it clung to her leg with an almost crushing strength. She winced and looked down, raising the sword again to strike it, and it turned its head to look up at her.

It was a little girl. The same, zombie-eyed, lifeless expression that haunted every face she'd seen, but, still, it was enough to give her pause.

"It's not going to hurt her," she whispered to herself, adjusting her grip to bring the sword down.

But something stopped her hand. Something cold as ice itself wrapped around her knuckles and stayed the blade.

Alys felt a chill run through her veins, and slowly she turned to come face-to-face with the Nightmare Queen herself.

The Nightmare might have been a beautiful creature were it not for the black and endless pools that had replaced her eyes. Her cheekbones were high and her lips were full as they pulled back into a terrifyingly familiar smile. Her fang-like teeth seemed to glow unnervingly white in the light of the vorpal blade, and, as they parted, she purred but two words. "Hello, Alys."

Alys's eyes widened.

Oswin froze in shock that the Nightmare knew her name. The hesitation cost him an all too precious moment, and he was overcome by the Possessed, who knocked him to the ground.

A wave of nauseating fear swept over Alys, from her core to her extremities, and it all came back to her. Charlie's suicide, the crooked house, the smell of cigarettes and vodka. The nightly screaming she'd fallen asleep to when she was young, the bruises she'd had to hide. She felt the thorns of roses tearing at her skin, and she felt the hands of strangers pulling her from her bed. She remembered tears streaming down her face, the pounding on the door the first time she'd bought a lock, and careening off the road in the rain. The fear that had been ripped from her memory overwhelmed her now in its devastating return.

"Mom?" Alys whispered in disbelief.

"It's time to say goodnight."

The sword shattered beneath their hands.

Chapter 18

WHERE ARE YOU GOING, ALYS?

"Alys!"

The sound of her name being yelled by someone in the distance echoed past her, but when she turned to look behind her, there was nothing but a long and empty hallway. She stared down the passage, half expecting someone to walk into view, but she wasn't sure who she was waiting for. Her head felt fuzzy.

What had she been doing?

Someone moved a few feet to the side of her, opening a large wooden cabinet that towered above them at a surreal height. Even with half of him hidden behind a large cabinet door, she knew him. From the way his jeans fell over his bizarrely pristine red Converse shoes to the matching red, hooded sweatshirt she could see peeking out around the hand that held the cabinet door open.

Alys smiled, never so glad to see him as she was in that moment. "Charlie?"

"Why did you let me do it, Alys?" he asked softly.

She hesitated. "What?"

The door closed slowly, and the familiar face looking back at her was struck with betrayal. "You knew something was wrong. Why didn't you say something? Why did you let me do it, Alys?"

She shook her head. "I--I didn't know."

"You could have stopped me."

"I would have, if..."

"Bullshit." He held out a handgun towards her, holding it by the barrel to encourage her to take the grip. "Take it."

Alys took a step back. "I don't want it."

"You don't want it," Charlie repeated mockingly. "You'll let me do the work for you, but you can't manage pulling a trigger on your own."

Alys looked from his face to the gun and back up again. "I...I didn't kill you, Charlie."

"Didn't you?"

Alys shook her head desperately. "No, I didn't do *anything*!"

The sneer that spread across her friend's face made him almost unrecognizable. "Same thing." He raised the gun again, this time pointing the barrel at her, and took a shot.

Alys cried out as a searing hot pain ripped through her shoulder. The force of the bullet pushed her backward, but she didn't fall to the ground. Instead, she fell down and down, twisting and turning until she plummeted onto a briar patch of white roses. She tried to push herself up, but the thorns bit into her skin anyway she moved.

She was bleeding, the red drops sliding down the stems and staining the white petals a deep crimson.

"See, Alyson?"

Alys recognized her mother's voice, and she craned her head upward to try and see her.

Lucy's arms were folded as she towered over her at an unnatural height. She shook her head again and again. "That's the color they should have been. That's the color I asked for."

Alys attempted to prop herself up with a hand, but it sunk through the bushes until her arm was submerged to her shoulder. The branches twisted, wrapping around her arm with a weight that seemed determined to pull the rest of her under. She could feel dozens of thorns piercing her, blood streaming down her arm to drip off her fingertips. "Mom!"

"Don't make such a racket, darling, the neighbors will hear you," Lucy chided.

"Help me," Alys begged, thrashing against the hold of the thorns to free her arm, tearing fabric and skin. "I'm stuck. I can't get out of here!" Her throat felt so tight she barely had the voice to shout.

"Out? You're not even half done."

"Mommy, please..."

"Don't cry, Alyson, it's pathetic. Can't you do anything right?"

"Don't leave!" Alys rolled onto her stomach, flinching as the thorns bit and scratched at every inch of exposed skin. She sat back on her knees and yanked on her arm, the fabric of her sweatshirt ripping as she tugged unrelentingly upward.

"Such a disappointment." She could hear footsteps retreating. "Always letting everyone down."

"Wait!" she pleaded, finally freeing her arm so she could push herself to her feet, taking a few frantic steps forward before falling through the floor of flowers and hitting the hardwood of the main entrance to the Lewis home.

Alys lay there, unmoving, her eyes half shut and unfocused. She felt the warmth first begin to leave her fingers, the cold starting its languid crawl up her extremities. She was going to die there, alone, bleed out, and the world would be better off. It wouldn't even notice.

Like she hadn't noticed Charlie.

Red converse shoes moved past her vision and started up the stairs.

Alys's eyes opened fully and as she rolled over and pushed herself up, the air suddenly feeling like molasses around her.

Charlie was already at the top of the stairs and moving away from her down the hall.

It was a fight against gravity itself as she gripped the railing, hoisting herself up each step as quickly as she could while the very air around her resisted each movement.

"You need to go faster," Charlie's voice advised.

Alys gritted her teeth as she hauled herself over the top step.

"You're not going to make it."

She threw herself into a run, and, for a full second, everything froze and she hung in midair like someone had pressed the pause button on the movie of her life. Then it released her and she broke into a sprint, suddenly unhindered by the air around her. She raced into the room as she had the last time she'd visited Charlie's house, the door banging loudly against the wall as she flung it open.

This time around, the room did not smell like Lysol, but *him*: that strange, unique smell that could only be defined to Alys as "Charlie." It was comforting and familiar, and, as she turned to look at the bed, she saw the gun in Charlie's mouth and her eyes focused on the trigger.

His finger tensed and she closed her eyes as the gunshot pierced her ears, feeling a spray of hot blood hitting her face.

"I didn't do anything!"

"Same thing."

At first, she wasn't sure if she was crying or if she was feeling the blood drops slipping down her cheeks. She didn't dare open her eyes, afraid of what she might see. Her mouth tightened, pressing her lips together firmly to keep either tears or blood out of her mouth.

"Don't cry, Alyson. It's pathetic."

She wiped frantically at her face with her sleeve and stood to run out into the hallway. She didn't look at anything until she knew his body would be out of sight. But as she ran, the hall grew longer and the walls stretched high above her.

"Where are you going, Alys?"

Shadows with fangs and glowing eyes loomed over her, and now, suddenly seven-years-old, she was climbing under her bed, pushing aside toys as she burrowed deeper under the frame and mattress. Her heart pounded in her chest, and she tried to quiet her breathing.

"Alyson, get out here," her mother called from down the hall "Where are you?"

She watched her door burst open and her

mother's high heels paced back and forth in front of her bed.

Doom-tek. Doom-tek. Doom-tek.

Alys held her breath.

The heels waited impatiently before retreating from view.

Alys exhaled in relief.

Something gripped her by the back of her hair and dragged her out from under the bed. "Are you hiding from me?"

Alys screamed and tried to break free from the hold her mother had on her, but her mother's nails only dug deeper into her scalp.

"Wicked, wretched girl. No wonder your father left us."

She flailed and clawed and pushed away, falling back onto the floor. She pushed herself up desperately, scrambling from the room as fast as she could.

Thunder clapped and the lights went out.

Lightning flashed and the rain began to fall.

She felt exhaustion sinking in as she pushed herself into a standing position, the ground muddy around her. She felt numb from the cold of the water as it quickly seeped through her clothing.

Lightning flashed again and the Nightmare stood before her on a rain-soaked battlefield.

"They're dying, Alys. Can you hear them cry?" the Nightmare whispered. Somehow her voice carried over the howling winds. It resonated in Alys' ears. Inescapable.

As the light danced over the terrain again, she saw the bodies. Doubled over each other, strewn about like rag dolls discarded by a child that had no more use for them.

"You left them, like you left everyone else."

The storm revealed only moments at a time of the horror that lay before them, but her imagination provided the details. She saw Robin crouched over Basir, her wings torn and bleeding as she clutched the body of the man she'd loved to her. Another beacon of light showed her Smoke's lifeless form reaching out uselessly to the crumpled body of Rosalind. The next shone light on Oswin lying on his back with a guard's halberd embedded in his chest, his eyes milky and glazed over.

"You selfish, wicked girl, what have you done?"

"It wasn't me," Alys whispered, sinking to her knees. "I swear. I did nothing."

"*Nothing* can be what matters in the end."

"It wasn't me," she repeated.

"You were the end of them," the Nightmare said solemnly. "If not for you, then Jack would be alive."

Lightning flashed again, but, instead of thunder in its wake, the sound of the executioner's axe echoed across the sky.

"If not for you, they would have come in time."

"I didn't mean to," Alys pleaded.

"Still, what's done is done."

"Please forgive me."

"For you, there can be none."

Charlie's shoes started up the stairs.

"The crimes that you commit in idleness…"

The sound of crashing bottles from the next room and voices shouting drowned out the sound of thunder.

"The lives that you destroyed upon your birth…"

The lightning lit the battlefield in all its terror, and she could not tear her eyes away from the lifeless gaze Oswin seemed to have fixed in her direction.

"And those that perished for your

selfishness prove you a plague that must be wiped from Earth."

Alys closed her eyes and started rocking slowly back and forth, murmuring over and over again, "Oh, god, please forgive me. I'm so sorry."

Boards lightly creaked as Charlie started up the stairs again.

She bent forward and wrapped her arms around herself, gripping so tightly that her knuckles whitened and her nails bit into her own arms. "Please don't. I'm begging, please. Don't leave again. I'm so sorry, Charlie, please forgive me. *Please* forgive me. Charlie, don't go. Don't go. I need you here. Please, *please* forgive me..."

"Hey, you." That voice.

Alys stopped and opened her eyes.

The storm had stopped.

The air was still.

Red sneakers stood before her.

She hesitated and unraveled herself enough to look at the boy standing in front of her, from the blond curls to the faint dusting of freckles across his nose. Something was different. The Nightmare was nowhere to be seen. She blinked, expecting him to accuse her again.

He smiled his crooked half-smile.

Alys shook her head slowly. "I didn't do anything."

"You didn't," he said. It wasn't an accusation.

"I'm sorry."

"Don't be."

"I don't understand…" Why wasn't he yelling at her? Why did his face seem so kind, so…so very unlike the nightmare that tormented her only moments before. "No, I don't expect you do. I wish I had the time to explain…"

"Please stop using him to torture me."

Charlie shook his head.

Alys buried her face in her hands. "You're not real," she whispered, sitting back on her heels. "You're not him. You're just one of her illusions."

Charlie crouched down carefully beside her and reached up a hand to gently stroke her hair. "Okay, sweetie, let's say I'm not real…I'm just in your head." He brought his other hand up to coax her chin up and cup her face in his hands. "But if *I'm* only in your head, then you know *all of this* is in your head."

Alys looked away.

"Why are you doing this to yourself? Why have you always done this to yourself? Even when we were kids you were blaming yourself for things that were completely out of your control."

"I should have been there for you."

"Alys, you *were* there for me." Charlie laughed incredulously. "Every minute of every day, I just had to *look* at the phone and you dropped everything to be there for me."

Her eyes were starting to well up with tears again. "Then why didn't I stop you? Why didn't I know how much you were hurting? Why didn't I know what you were going to do?"

"Because that's life," he offered with a small shrug. "It's a bitch. It's not a movie. There's no musical score change or magical psychic connection or whatever. You don't always know when the bad parts are going to happen, but that doesn't make you a bad person. It doesn't make you self-centered."

"But I could have prevented it," she protested.

"No, Alys, you couldn't have." Charlie's hands dropped from her face to her shoulders. "Please, believe that, if nothing else, I need you to believe me when I say this: *There was nothing you could have done.*"

Her throat felt tight and she looked down to gain her composure, but, failing that, she simply asked. "Why not?"

"I didn't want to be helped," he answered softly. "I had already decided I was beyond saving, and I wasn't going to hear any differently from anyone." He brushed the hair from her face and shook his head. "You've got to stop blaming yourself. For me, for why your father left, for your mother's alcoholism. There was *nothing* you could have done, okay?"

"But—"

"Your parents made a choice. *I* made a choice. And we did it without any encouragement from you." His brow furrowed. "And if you keep torturing yourself like this, if you keep blaming yourself for things you can't control—for things you will never be able to control--you're going to end up like *me*. Is that what you want? Thinking the only way out of this hell is to end everything?"

Alys held her breath uncomfortably, looked down and then away from him. Finally, she let out a long, exasperated sigh. "No." She rubbed her face. "I don't want that. I don't want anything like that."

"...It's okay to be mad at me."

"What?" Alys dropped her hands to meet his eyes. "Charlie, I'm not mad at you."

"You are, and you feel guilty for it." He smiled a little. "It's okay. I'd probably be mad at me, too. I...*am* a little mad at me. But I'm trying to make good on that now."

She shook her head and reached out to hold his hands. "I'm not mad at you."

"Alys, I left you alone. I left you alone with your *mother*. I took all our plans of getting out of there together and I threw them out the window like they didn't matter. I didn't tell you what was going on with me. I didn't tell Brian or anyone else, and the only thing I left you with--the only bit of comfort I even attempted to give you--was a tiny piece of paper instructing my parents to make my apologies to you for me. And you're telling me you're okay with that? You expect me to believe that my best friend in the whole world, Miss Always-Has-a-Snarky-Comeback, isn't the slightest bit mad I didn't even attempt to do more?"

Alys started to cry again, and her grip tightened on his hands, knowing it was nothing more than her own imagination fueling the sensation of the warmth of his palms. "It's selfish of me to think that."

"No, Alys. It was selfish of me to leave. It was selfish of me to refuse to take my medication or to see my doctor to treat my condition because I thought the only reason my mother made me go was to 'un-gay' me. You are more than allowed to be angry that I left and didn't even try to say a proper goodbye. I'd be shocked if you weren't angry with me." He leaned his forehead against hers. "You were always pushing for better for us. I wish I'd listened."

"It's okay," Alys whispered. "I don't listen when I talk, either." They both laughed a little.

"I've missed our little talks," Charlie murmured.

"Me, too," Alys answered, her throat feeling tight again. "More than you will ever know. I feel so lost without you."

Charlie's eyes softened. "I know. But you're going to find your way out of the woods. I know it's dark now, but there's a light out there waiting for you. You just have to find it inside yourself."

"Inside myself." Alys laughed bitterly.

"You're a good person, Alys. I know you're a good person. *You* know you're a good person."

"I don't know that."

"Alys," Charlie whispered with a wry, if not cocky, smile. "You said I am you, remember? So, by your logic, you already know all of this somewhere in the back of your mind. And, for a little while there, you even *believed* it."

"Because I didn't know any better. They did something to my memory. I didn't know. I didn't--"

"You didn't have that stupid little voice in your head to tell you differently," Charlie corrected her. "For the first time ever, you were comfortable in your own skin. You didn't have years of your mother's abuse pushing you down."

"It wasn't real."

"Why? Because you didn't have all of this emotional baggage weighing you down? You don't have to forget it to let go of it, Alys. For the love of god, just let go of it. You're better than this."

Alys shook her head. "I know you don't want to believe me, kiddo, but I need you to. Everyone is depending on it. So please…one last time, I need you to trust me."

"I wish you were here."

"I'm here now."

Alys sniffled and shook her head. "You know what I mean." She took a deep breath and looked at her nails, thinking this over. "I feel so alone."

"I know, love, but you aren't alone."

"What am I supposed to do without you?"

Charlie simply smiled. "Be happy."

Alys looked behind her to where the battlefield had been only minutes before. "How? I've ruined everything."

"These visions are only what she wants you to see, not what actually is. There's still time to set this right."

"If I even can."

"*You can*. Nightmares only have the power you give them. If you're not afraid, what can they actually do?"

Alys opened her mouth to answer, but stopped, finding herself at a loss for a retort. "I don't even know where to begin."

Charlie fixed her with an intense look as if trying to convey something he could not say aloud. "Try to think of all of this like a game of *chess*."

Alys paused. It was a suggestion that truly epitomized Charlie, but never one she'd ever give herself. Her face clouded over in confusion. "I'm no good at chess."

"Sure, you are." Charlie slowly rose to stand. "Just remember everything I taught you." He offered his hand to help her up. "And try to think a few moves ahead."

Alys took a deep breath and took his hand.

Chapter 19

CHECKMATE

Oswin rolled to the side just as a halberd came down hard to the left of him, sinking into the ground. He looked up at the guard attempting to pry the weapon loose and kicked his feet into the guard's gut, knocking him backwards. It at least bought him enough time to get to his feet again. He turned and used the pommel of the blade to clock another man square in the jaw, sending him back against the rose hedges.

The guard slumped to the ground, unconscious. Oswin squinted ahead and saw the shards of the sword strewn around the platform.

Within the circle of mirror shards, the Nightmare had released Alys's now unarmed hand and placed her own on the Dreamer's forehead, sending a dark cloud around her form.

"Alys!" Oswin tried to shout over the noise around him, but if she could hear him, she wasn't responding. He pushed through the crowd, sheathing his sword and tying the binding around it so he could use the weapon as a bludgeon, at worst injuring those still possessed rather than dealing fatal wounds. "Alys, you have to snap out of it!"

Fingers clawed and bit at him, trying to drag him back to the ground as the enemy crowded around him. He tried to ward them away by swinging the sheathed sword, but he was losing room to pull back his arm enough for momentum. His back bumped up against the rose hedge, and he knew he'd run out of room to run.

"Oswin!" a voice called over the noise, and, while not the woman he'd been calling for, a small flame of relief flickered through him when he saw Rosalind. "Hold your breath!"

A plume of dust and smoke curled out above their heads and, instinctively, Oswin held a hand over his nose and mouth. The dust fell on the crowd that surrounded him and they closed their eyes and fell to the ground as if suddenly overcome by sleep.

Smoke dropped from his perch on top of the hedge, shifting from cat to human upon landing on the ground. "Little trick I learned in my days with Oberon," he explained. "They'll be out for a while."

Unhindered by Oswin's pursuers, Rosalind moved to stand beside Smoke. "The castle is completely overrun with them. I don't think there's a single person still in possession of their own mind in there."

"No full corruptions, though," Smoke explained. "She's not strong enough to create Jabberwocks, thank the night."

"I'm just glad you're okay," Oswin breathed.

Rosalind smiled. "You, too."

"We'll have time for that when some of us actually are okay," Smoke dismissed them. "We saw the Army from the castle. Did you bring the sword?"

Oswin swallowed. The sword. "We did..."

"Where is it?"

Oswin just looked past them at the platform where the only creature left standing towered over Alys, both contained in a swirling tempest of darkness.

Alys sank to her knees, and the shadows that moved around her began to grow and separate from the main cloud, forming strange and terrible creatures. They held no solid form, but the shifting image seemed to suggest something akin to large horned dogs.

"Shit." Smoke grabbed Rosalind by the arm and pushed her towards the exit. "We need to run."

"What?" Oswin asked, able only to glance at Smoke before his eyes snapped back to the guard dogs who now stalked around the platform, staring down the small party like a pack of wolves. He couldn't even see Alys through the cloud around her anymore, which was now casting more shadows—different shadows, none quite like the other.

They were unnatural: limbs long and slender and nearly spider-like. They had the semblance of human faces with nightmarish additions. They crawled and hissed and slid like snakes. Some carried weapons, while others were weapons enough on their own. They were spiked and fanged and clawed, and they had toxins oozing from their pores.

The Nightmare had found a way to raise her army, and she drew it out of hell itself.

"We have to get out of here, Your Highness, without the vorpal blade. There's nothing we can do against her now," Smoke explained urgently. "She's going to bleed Alys dry of every horrible thought she can fathom."

Oswin hesitated, looking from his sword to the platform as the dogs slowly slunk down the steps and towards them. "We can't just leave her here." He quickly untied the binding on his sword. "I *won't*."

"Oswin!" Rosalind yelled as Smoke tried to lead her towards the courtyard's entrance into the hedge maze.

Oswin drew his sword again. He might not be able to kill them, but these creatures at least he could fight without fear of harming one of his own citizens. "I *will not* leave her."

The dogs snarled.

Smoke growled in frustration and turned to Rosalind, pushing the sleeping dust into her hands. "Take this and go."

Rosalind shook her head. "Silas, I —"

"Your sense of loyalty is moving, my dear, but I will not let us both be idiots today. You're a diplomat, not a soldier. You have no place here." He cradled her face in his hands and kissed her softly. "Go. Find somewhere safe, if you can."

She lingered for one stubborn moment before vanishing into the hedge maze heading back towards the city.

"You and I are going to have a very long talk when this is over," Oswin said, eyeing Smoke like a brother might size up his sister's boyfriend.

"Your Highness, I will be more than happy to discuss my intentions towards your cousin if we actually make it out of this alive." He pauses, and adds with a wry smile. "Then again, considering we're probably going to die in the next five minutes, there's a good chance I'm lying." Smoke took off in a run towards the dogs, shifting once more into the large cat. He launched onto one of the creatures, sinking his teeth into its neck. It howled in pain, which seemed to alert the other nightmares.

Oswin drew his sword back, making an upward crescent cut that caught one of the dogs across the neck, sending it whining and rolling a foot or two along the ground. They bled a greenish-black ooze that corroded the stone within seconds of touching it.

A small ball of fire shot across the courtyard and hit one of the spider-like nightmares and then another. From over the hedge, Robin shot arrow after arrow, lighting each with her magic before she released it.

Shortly after, Basir, rapier in hand, emerged from the hedge maze and joined Oswin at his side.

"Glad you could make it," Oswin offered, narrowly dodging a spike thrown by one of the nightmares that had just pulled themselves from the growing cloud around Alys and the Nightmare Queen.

"Your mother would never forgive me if I'd acted with disregard to my conscience," Basir answered, sticking the point of his blade so deep in the heart of one of the creatures that he had to push it away with his foot in order to retrieve it. "Though, I confess, my sense of reason would have me do otherwise."

"You wouldn't be yourself if it didn't, old friend," Oswin mused through gritted teeth.

The onslaught pressed on against them, and, while they kept up a good fight, they knew it was a losing battle with far too many opponents to conquer and no blade capable of dealing the final blow.

And then, suddenly, as if via a gust of wind, the shadow around Alys cleared and the nightmares paused.

The Nightmare opened her eyes and her smile faded as her gaze slowly dropped to her stomach where Alys had placed her hand, unnoticed.

Alys slowly raised her bowed head and pulled her hand back sharply, drawing a blade from the Nightmare as if it had been sheathed there all along. It was thinner in design than the first, and the hilt far more splendid in its architecture, but, nonetheless, it still possessed one name: vorpal blade.

Oswin breathed a sigh of relief, his free hand idly gripping at his heart as if it had started beating again for the first time since she went under the Nightmare's spell.

The Nightmare took a few uncertain steps backward, her black eyes fixed on the

Dreamer. How had this happened? For years Alys had crumpled under these visions.

Alys spun the sword above her head, and, as she did, the blade's glow began to pulse. "Wanna know a secret?" She brought her sword down, the glowing energy spreading out like a ripple in a pond. It burned through every dark creature her mind had spawned like they were no more than air.

Now finding herself quite outnumbered, the Nightmare took another step back.

"I know what you're afraid of." Alys met the Nothing in her eyes head on and smiled at it.

The Nightmare clenched the long fingers of her right hand together and they slowly extended, melding together until they created a blade of their own.

Alys took a deep breath. "Try to think a few moves ahead," she whispered Charlie's words to herself. "It's like *chess*."

The Nightmare thrust her own blade low, and, much to her own surprise, Alys parried it. The Nightmare arched upward to cut at Alys's neck, and, again, only met the vorpal blade.

Alys exhaled something that sounded halfway between a laugh and a breath of relief. She wasn't sure if it was the blade, or if somehow Charlie himself was guiding her hand, but it moved smoothly through the air, matching every attack the Nightmare threw at her.

"You think that you can beat me? Think again," the Nightmare said and, only a few feet away, Oswin flinched. The cadence of her voice coaxed his heart to beat in time with it.

"No pretty words and no magic rhythms," Alys countered as her sword did the same. "No rhymes to capture peasant, prince or king."

"I am a Queen. You are a frightened girl," the Nightmare snarled, her swings becoming more furious.

"Bind up your tongue for silence is the thing," Alys countered.

The Nightmare opened up her mouth to curse at her, but, though wind passed over her tongue and through her lips, no sound emerged. She startled, her eyes widening in panic. Alys had stripped away her language using her own game against her.

Alys thrust her sword back into the very spot she'd originally drawn it, which forced the Nightmare to her knees.

When she retracted the sword, the Nightmare fell forward, holding her left hand to the wound, which seeped out dark crimson liquid. It dripped onto the white marble as it had during Jack's execution.

"The land will mend where it was ripped apart. May she no longer reign as Queen of Hearts." Alys reached out and removed the White Queen's crown from the Nightmare's head before she sank her fingers into the roots of her hair and pulled back so her neck was fully exposed. "Her fate sealed by the fear and blood she spread." She drew the blade up, which crackled furiously at its proximity to the Nightmare. "And with the vorpal blade... off...with her head." The sword swung and cleanly separated the head from her shoulders, the lifeless body falling back to the marble platform with a thud that made Alys's stomach churn.

She watched the blood spreading out seemingly without end until it pooled off the edge, dropping down on the roses below.

Alys dropped the head in disgust, and, as she did, it melted into the blood until all traces of both the head and the actual body was no more. Her breath shuddered. She took a few shaky steps off the platform and was met by Oswin, who caught her as she stumbled, and held her to him tightly.

"It's okay. I got you," Oswin murmured.

"I think I'm gonna throw up," Alys said.

Robin dropped down from where she had been flying over the hedge, carefully looping her arm through her bow. "Is that all of them?"

"I think so." Basir sheathed his sword and breathed a sigh of relief. "It's finally over."

Smoke circled towards the courtyard entrance, his brow furrowed as he changed from feline to humanoid in a wispy cloud of smoke. "If it's over, why does it sound like the fighting is still going on out there?"

The group looked to each other before wordlessly moving towards the city.

Rosalind was waiting for them as they exited the hedge maze.

"I thought I said go somewhere safe," Smoke said, a wry smile tugging at his lips.

Rosalind turned to look at him, but didn't share his amusement for the situation. "I was going to sneak out through the side streets of the city when I found him." She stepped aside to show the once great King Erebus still huddled over like a beaten dog, aged far beyond his years, weak and trembling.

"Father?" Oswin carefully broke away from Alys to kneel by the man, gently resting his hands on his shoulders.

"You both couldn't have found somewhere safe?" Smoke asked Rosalind, a slight edge to his voice.

"I don't understand. Why is he still like this?" Oswin asked, trying to look the seemingly blind man in the eyes and see if he could manage any kind of response from him.

"That's not all," Rosalind said, nodding towards where the path to the city dipped downward enough to offer a view of the city square. As the battle came into view, it drew more questions than answers. Fae and Dream fought alongside each other, but they were still fighting back citizens of the city, still possessed by The Nightmare's spell.

"Where did they all come from? They should be free—back in control of themselves." Robin murmured. "You defeated the Queen..."

There was something in Robin's voice that rang in Alys' ears as she watched the war raging below them, something she'd nearly forgotten, and, suddenly, Charlie's words about chess took on a far different meaning. Her eyes widened, finally understanding what exactly he'd been trying to tell her. "Because defeating the Queen isn't a checkmate. You don't need her to win..."

"What?" Robin asked.

"She was a decoy." Alys turned slowly towards King Erebus and Oswin. "Isn't that right, Your Highness?" Her eyes narrowed, her heartbeat quickening. "Classic misdirection. It was Charlie's favorite move in chess: setting up the Queen to take the fall."

Oswin looked from Alys to his father, who turned his sightless eyes slowly towards Alys.

The king's mouth twisted into a cruel kind of smirk, and he straightened his back until he stood at his full height again. The age melted away in one smooth movement and the milky blue eyes came into focus until they were capable of fixing a cold stare on Alys. He clapped slowly. "Very good, Alys," he congratulated her patronizingly. "Perhaps that little worm taught you something, after all."

"Who are you?" Oswin took a step back from the king, not recognizing the face that wore his father's crown.

But Alys did. It was the same face that adorned paintings in the Lewis home and the main hall of the town gun club. It was the one face her best friend feared. A face that Charlie might have, much to his own horror, begun mirroring one day. "You're Charlie's nightmare."

"How is that even possible?" Oswin asked.

"It's possible, my boy," the king answered with a slow and slimy smile. "Because your father was tired of living under your mother's shadow and I provided that possibility. I embodied *power*. With that power he could help shift the tides of your pathetic little war."

"Erebus would never make a deal with a Nightmare," Rosalind insisted.

The Nightmare King looked to her. "Desperation makes fools of us all, my dear." The

Nightmare King was starting to look less like Mr. Lewis as Alys had known him. His features began to twist and distort into how Charlie must have seen him in his sleep. "He had such *hope*, your king. He thought he would be able to use us, that he would be able to resist the inevitable. Poor fool. I will grant him, it did take quite some time... He managed to keep our influence at bay for many years."

"Then it was King Erebus opened the door to The Nothing? *He* released the Horror?" Robin whispered.

"That's why there was no struggle at The Door," Smoke said. "It was their king approaching. They completely trusted him. They had no reason to suspect anything was wrong."

"Nor my mother," Oswin realized, his throat feeling dry.

"I will not listen to slander, Nightmare." Basir drew his own sword. "Your poison tongue has tainted the air too long." He lunged, thrusting quick and low, but the Nightmare King caught the blade with his hand.

The steel sliced through the skin of the Nightmare King's hand like butter, but his grip offered enough resistance that it stopped short of piercing his midsection. He watched the way his own blood gushed through his fingers and onto the sword, and, for a moment, seemed utterly unconcerned. Then he stepped towards Basir and pushed the sword back into him with unnatural strength, throwing both the man and his weapon to the ground.

Basir coughed, the pommel of the blade having dug into his gut, knocking the wind out of him. He tried to sit up and immediately raised the sword again to defend himself—only to find that half of the blade had melted from the corrosive blood that now covered it.

The Nightmare King's nose scrunched up ever so slightly with a wicked little smile, like he'd found the whole attempt on his life to be no more than a cute little joke. He waggled a finger, playfully shaming Basir while the wound he'd inflicted sealed itself up again. "I will tell you the merge was exhilarating! Well worth my years of patience. The strength it gave me, *the things I could control...*" He looked to Alys and grinned like someone who'd just consumed an enormous dinner. "And, of course, when I *won* Charlie…"

Alys felt her blood boil. "You *killed* Charlie."

"And you can't imagine what power that triumph gave me." The Nightmare King's grin widened. "His death was the perfect burst of power for getting a hold of *your* little creation. I had *hoped* that Queen Aislynn would have been more susceptible to corruption, but your Horror suited just fine. Nasty piece of work, you thought up. She made a good front. She was a clever puppet, much like you, I suppose."

"I am no one's puppet," Alys seethed. She raised her sword again.

The Nightmare King stepped away from Basir and walked towards the blade, circling Alys just outside of her reach. "Now this *is* intriguing. You've seen what I can do, and yet you would rather fight? Even with all your fears returned. Even after everything that's happened. Aren't you tired, Alys?"

She held her ground and angled her wrist more so the sword was held level to his throat.

"Do you know what I am, little girl?"

"Jabberwock," Alys breathed.

Scales erupted rapidly over skin, which

burst into huge leathery wings and poison spikes. In a manner of moments, the creature she'd seen sketched at the Phrontistery stood before her in all its terror. Tendrils of smoke rose out of its nose, and it fixed its all too clever eyes on her as if smug with itself. "Are you afraid yet, Dreamer? I will draw every nightmare from your mind until you no longer have the strength to live."

Alys swallowed and took a few steps back, raising the sword higher. She looked down at the blade in her hand and then sized up the Jabberwock's stature. She could never fight him here. She wasn't even sure she could fight him at all. He was nearly ten times her size! Her mind raced. She had to get the Jabberwock out of the city. There were too many people, and their weapons would be useless against him, just like Basir's.

Beware the Jabberwock, my son, the jaws that bite, the claws that catch...

How had Rosalind said Morpheus defeated the Nightmares? Lopped off its head and sealed it with the nightmares behind The Door...The *Door.* She glanced behind her and then looked to the others, meeting Oswin's eyes. She swallowed, mouthed, *Trust me*. She raised her gaze to meet the beast's, her breathing leveling out. "You want your army, Nightmare? Come and get it." She turned and ran into the city streets.

The Jabberwock made a horrible screeching noise that could only be described as laughter. "Where are you going, Alys?" He flapped his large wings, pushing himself high into the air. The creature followed her as she fled down the winding streets of Elan Vital, avoiding the center so she wouldn't be hindered by the ongoing battle.

Oswin started after her, but was stopped by Robin. "What are you doing? You can't fight. You don't even have a weapon that will work against it. The last thing Terra Mirum needs is to lose another ruler. Are you crazy?"

"Are *you* crazy? I can't let her do this alone."

"After seeing what that girl is capable of, I'm pretty sure she can handle it without you," Robin said.

"That doesn't mean she has to." Oswin pulled his arm away and started after them.

The Jabberwock breathed green fire and Alys ducked under a roof to avoid it. The flames smelled like sulfur, and when a burning piece of roof fell, she noticed it seemed to be simultaneously corroding, like it had touched acid along with being eaten up by the flame.

Alys tried to zigzag her run so she was harder to hit, but she found herself still just narrowly dodging each pillar of flame that fell down upon her. The city had barriers she could duck behind, but she would be all on her own once she broke into the field that separated Elan Vital from Thought. She had to get to The Door.

The Jabberwock swooped down and snapped at her as she fled her last cover, making a break for the forest she could see in the near distance.

Alys turned just in time to swing the sword upward and catch the beast under his jaw, sending him recoiling backward. The ground rumbled beneath her when the creature hit the ground, having been too low to pull back up after her attack. She knew he was far from beaten, but the stumble would buy her time.

The Jabberwock screamed in fury and drops of corrosive blood burned into the earth as it pushed itself off the ground again and into the air where she could not reach him.

Alys could feel the intense heat from another wave of flames as she barely escaped through the thickly knit trees and into the forest. She was starting to worry—the roots and trees slowed her down, and the Jabberwock was relentlessly setting fire to everything its breath could reach. It started high above her and drops of flame and acid fell around her onto the forest floor.

"You can't hide forever."

Alys remembered Smoke coaching her to shrink, and tried to remember where her mind had gone. She'd been desperate. She'd wanted it—no, she'd *needed* it to happen—and, as she broke through the city gates and out onto the paths of Thought, she focused on that with all her might. She'd never been more desperate than she was now. *Get to The Door. Get to The Door.*

"Still a frightened little girl with nowhere to go," the Jabberwock taunted. "I'm going to shatter every last inch of your sanity."

She thought about Charlie in the forest leading her to The Nothing. She thought about him coming to her at the very exact moment she needed him in her fight against the Nightmare. She leapt over roots and pushed off stumps as she heard the trees behind her falling.

The Jabberwock wouldn't be able to tell where she was going from up there. If she managed to keep up the pace, she stood a chance.

"Come on, come on," Alys whispered. "Almost there, almost there." She could see the clearing.

Fire poured down like a waterfall as she passed through the sparser trees, and Alys hissed as splashes of the corrosive material hit the skin on her arm. She took two steps backward and the Jabberwock landed between her and The Door to The Nothing.

His tail swished and splintered two trees to the side of him. "I'm growing impatient with playing cat and mouse."

Alys's heart pounded. She could see gnarled tree and The Door wedged in the trunk just beyond the Jabberwock, but she was never going to be able to reach it with him standing in her path. Her grip tightened on the hilt of the vorpal blade. She could never open it from here.

The sword began to almost hum in her hand, and she looked from it to The Door. Alys' eyes widened. She could see a glimmer of light around the frame as if it were responding to the blade's power. "Okay," Alys agreed. "How about a joke?" She raised the hilt of the vorpal blade and the stone began to glow. "Knock-knock?"

"What?" The Jabberwock turned his head in time to see the door flung open behind him, the screams from before howling loudly as hands reached for anything they could pull in — and they began pulling on his tail. He dug his claws into the ground. He snapped out with his teeth, knocking the blade from Alys's hand before snapping at her pant leg to drag her with him towards The Nothing.

Alys kicked her feet into his snout and tried to grab at tree roots and weeds, anything she could use as leverage. The screams filled her ears and she felt nauseated. They beckoned to her darker thoughts, and her energy split between fighting them and the

Jabberwock's pull. "You are not taking me too!" She grasped desperately at one of the large roots just out of her reach.

"Alys!" Oswin broke through the trees and drew his sword, bringing it down on the creature's snout, embedding it deep into the armored scales.

The Jabberwock cried out, releasing Alys as the blood bubbling up from the wound melted Oswin's blade. In a matter of seconds, the corroded sword fell uselessly to the ground, having been severed in two by the corrosive liquid. It caused the smallest of recoils within the Jabberwock, but it was enough that the hands that gripped at him pulled him deeper into The Nothing with a horrible shriek.

"Close the door!" Alys yelled.

Oswin kicked his now useless blade out of his way and moved to push the great door shut.

The Jabberwock's nose pushed out against it, and then the hands that had been reaching to pull things in now also wrapped around the door to push it open again to draw more into the abyss.

Alys scrambled to her feet, scooping up

the fallen vorpal blade. "This is for Charlie," she growled, chopping at the Jabberwock's snout where Oswin's mark was now fast healing. It created a long gash that seemed to burn into the scales of the beast.

The Jabberwock screeched and vanished into the darkness of the pawing shadow hands.

Alys immediately slammed her shoulder into the door beside Oswin. The two dug their heels into the dirt, pushing against it with all of their might. "Come on…so close…"

And then Alys felt someone else behind her, a hand laying over her other shoulder, giving her the extra push needed to lock the door in place.

"Checkmate!" she sighed in relief, but when she turned to see who else had joined them, she saw no one. Her brow furrowed slightly and she rubbed her shoulder, the phantom pressure that had been there just moments before still clear in her recollection.

Oswin was leaning on the door, the exhaustion finally getting to him. "Are you all right?"

"Yeah…" Alys turned to face him. "It's just… for a moment there, I thought…I mean, I could have sworn I felt..." She shook her head and reached out to him. "Let's get back to the castle."

Chapter 20

The Hero of Terra Mirum

Elan Vital was in shambles. Not a single building in the main square remained untouched. Some suffered just burn damage, but the majority had stones crumbling off them or were barely recognizable in the rubble. Most of the people had survived the onslaught of the previous night, and those who hadn't were being given burials the following morning. The wounded stayed within the protective walls of the castle where they were tended to by anyone able to stand. The city was tired and haggard, but, finally, it was completely free of the Nightmares.

Alys should have been celebrating with the rest of them. They'd begged her to attend as their honored guest, but she'd been far too tired. She'd fallen asleep until late the following afternoon, long after all of the jubilations had died down. She wandered through the silent halls almost timidly, hoping to run into a familiar face. She finally found one in a small library in the East Hall, though he was more preoccupied with whatever he saw out the window and down below. "Hey."

Smoke turned a wide but charming grin in her direction. "So the great hero lives, after all. We'd started to worry you'd passed on in the middle of the night."

"Shut up." Alys smiled a little and stood beside him at the window. "What are you looking at?"

He nodded to the garden below where they'd fought the Nightmare Queen less than twenty-four hours prior. "The roses."

Alys looked at him and then followed his gaze. "They're red," she stated in surprise.

"They were like that this morning. There's nothing on them. They just changed."

"That doesn't make any sense."

Smoke chuckled. "Maybe in your world it doesn't. That ground is burdened with a heavy history now. It's seen the lives of both sides perish. The roses will be a reminder of what happened long after everything else has been repaired and rebuilt."

Alys nodded, and a silence fell between them as both pondered the battle they had barely survived.

"When do you leave?" His voice was soft.

"I don't know." She looked at him cautiously. "When do you?"

Smoke's mouth tightened into a thin line and he exhaled slowly through his nose, causing the window to temporarily fog over. "Few days. Oberon is going to help with initial repairs and I'll head back with him."

"For what it's worth, he did agree to help for the sake of his people. He may not seem so bad these days," Alys offered half-heartedly.

"No, I suppose not..." Smoke agreed, sounding surprised with himself. "And I think this whole ordeal may have worked to improve him. But a master, regardless how kind or fair, is still a *master*."

Alys frowned and fell silent.

He looked at her from the corner of his eye. "Robin tells me you may have had a great deal to do with his participation last night. That you were responsible for rallying that loyalty to his own people. Apparently, you were quite impressive."

Alys smiled a little, sheepishly looking down at her feet. "The more I think about it, the more I realize how absolutely reckless and stupid it actually was." She nudged his leg with her foot. "Will you be all right? Because I do have a whole new vorpal blade we could try to buy him off with."

He laughed. "I will be fine, Alys. There's no reason to lose any sleep over me. I did choose this. Despite being sworn to him, I'm told it will be different. And, besides, it may be nice to have semi-honest work again. I won't be living in the palace this time, so that will allow some considerable freedom I never had before. And it will be nice to see Titania again. She's the closest thing I've ever known to a mother. And Rosalind will even be joining me in a few months after Elan Vital is repaired and Oswin has settled in as King. So all things considered, I have few complaints."

Alys raised her eyebrows. "*Really*?"

Smoke flashed his usual grin. "Really."

"Huh..." She turned back towards the window. "Well done, there."

"Thank you."

Alys breathed on the window and drew a smiley face. She watched it evaporate as quickly as she'd drawn it. "Can I ask you something?"

"Yes, that really is not good for the window," Smoke said. "The maids will hate you for it."

Alys rolled her eyes with a smile. "I'm serious."

"You have yet to actually ask me anything, Dreamer."

"How much did you lie to me since I arrived?"

Smoke paused, mildly struck by the question. "Lie," he said, "is a very strong word to use, I think, depending on your definition."

"To conceal truthful information either by misdirection, misinformation, or omission in order to convey that a statement or concept of fiction is fact."

"Ah..." He nodded and scratched the back of his neck. "Well, quite a bit, then, I must confess."

"That's what I thought."

"For what it's worth, it was nothing personal."

"No, I know. You were trying to keep me from being a threat, I get it. I mean, for a minute there, I was quite literally a night-mare factory...I just..." Alys bit her lower lip. "I was curious if the part about seeing Charlie was a lie."

Smoke took a long pause and peered at her from the corner of his eye as if sizing up her question. "Honestly, Alys? I don't actually know."

Alys looked at him, not sure if he was yet again spinning her a tale.

"We may not live by your world's rules, but we don't have all the answers. We know the dead often hold a connection to our world, and that, somehow, they use it to reach out to loved ones while they dream, but...where they reside?" He shrugged a little and shook his head. "There are legends about the valley of the dead being just beyond The Nothing, but no one knows for sure. *Could* The Noth-ing have taken advantage of how susceptible you were to nightmares to draw you to it?

Yes. Is it also possible Charlie was there and was trying to lead you to where all this hell started?" The corner of his mouth hinted at a smile. "I certainly think so."

Alys returned the smile. "Me, too..."

"Alys?" Oswin poked his head into the room and stopped. "Sorry, am I interrupting? I was on my way to check on you when I heard your voice."

Smoke waggled his eyebrows at Alys and she hit his arm. He turned his classically toothy grin on Oswin. "Does this mean you're done monopolizing my fiancé for the time being?"

Oswin tried, and failed, not to look irked at this question. "So that is happening, is it?"

"I'm afraid so," the other man replied in mock solemnity.

"I'd still like to have a chat with you about that."

"I'm beginning to think you don't approve of me," Smoke teased. "And after all I did for you."

"After all you lied about," Oswin added.

"And I had my reasons," Smoke answered, then, to Alys with a smile, "People are so particular about honesty today, it's a little disturbing."

"You told me no pages were missing from Alys's memory."

"And they weren't." Smoke shrugged, giving Alys a wink. "Of course, I may have ripped out a few of the particularly nasty memories and replaced them with pages from a knight of Arthur's court who drank Lethe water—but the book did have the right number of pages."

"Oh, that explains a lot," Alys murmured, in realization, finally putting a place to the memories that seemed so out of sync with everything else. "I was wondering why I was so fixated on the glory of battle..."

"Plus, bonus, now you know how to wield a sword without ever having taken lessons," Smoke pointed out with a wide grin, but Oswin wasn't having any of it. He sighed. "She has all of her memories back now, so what's the problem?"

"You *lied* to me?" Oswin offered, folding his arms in disapproval.

"Yes, and I *did* feel terrible about that, really." Smoke nodded sincerely as he approached Oswin. "But, then, I remem-bered I didn't actually care and, so, I forgave myself." He gave Oswin a friendly but strong slap on the back. "I'll leave you two to talk, if you'll excuse me. I have a duchess to woo." He stopped and tipped an imaginary hat. "I'll miss you, Alys. It was a pleasure that I hope we have again."

"You too, Silas," Alys called after him.

Oswin watched him go and turned back to look at Alys with an exasperated sigh.

"Don't look at me--he's your future family." Alys put her palms up, washing her hands of the whole thing.

"Only by marriage," Oswin answered wryly.

Alys just smiled at him.

Oswin bit his lower lip and looked around as if expecting others were hiding in the room. "Do you have a minute?"

"Several, in fact."

He reached out his hand to her, fingers wiggling ever so slightly, like a child eager to hold something again. "Walk with me?"

Alys took it and laced her fingers through his as they left the library to stroll the halls together. It was a nice walk, and they were comfortable with the silence they fell into for the first few corridors. It didn't need conversation, but it snuck in anyway.

"How are you feeling?"

"Like I could still sleep for days," Alys confessed, swinging their arms between them. "And you?"

"Same." Oswin nodded, bringing up his free hand to wipe at his face as if the exhaustion could be brushed off his skin like the rain. "Rosalind has been walking me through all of my new duties with the help of Robin and Basir. In times of crisis, the king needs to remain constant so his people are reassured in the future they are rebuilding."

"That's right." Alys remembered. "You're a *king* now..." She laughed and shook her head.

"Is that funny?"

"No, I...it's just I hadn't gotten used to even thinking of you as a *prince* yet."

"You don't have to think of me as either, you know."

Alys looked at him and gave his hand a squeeze.

Oswin cleared his throat and looked at the design in the marble floor. "I'm told the train is ready to take you back to your home."

"Oh." Alys chewed her lower lip thoughtfully. "That soon?"

Oswin frowned.

"Ah." She nodded slowly. "I was hoping..."

"As was I."

Alys leaned her head on his shoulder and closed her eyes, the weight of this information sinking down and making her feet heavy.

Oswin rested his cheek on her head. "So, what will the hero of Terra Mirum do now?"

Alys laughed. "The Hero of Terra Mirum."

"Not my words," Oswin promised. "I'm afraid you've earned yourself quite the reputation around these parts. You're a bit of a legend."

"Apparently." She thought a moment. What would she do? She hadn't really planned that out before she left, and now that things had changed? She still didn't know. "Well, I still need to tell Brian about Charlie, and after that..." She held her breath a moment as if it would help her think, and then let out a long, exasperated exhale. "I don't know, get a job, scrounge out some kind of life in Seattle? I'll figure something out. Seems so…mundane now." It didn't sound very appealing, even to her. Her thumb traced circles on the center of his palm. "I suppose staying here would be out of the question."

She felt the muscles in his face tighten where they rested on her forehead. "Basir informs me having a Dreamer living among us would create a volatile environment with uncertain consequences."

"Always the optimist, that Basir."

"He's looking out for my people. It's what we pay him for."

"And you?"

"And I…" Oswin lifted his head from hers. "I wish this was something I could be selfish about, but I can't. There are more important things than what I want…"

"Heavy is the head that wears the crown," Alys observed. She tried to shrug the matter off unsuccessfully. "I wouldn't know how to live a life of honor and glory anyway."

"I think you were born for greater things than you give yourself credit for."

Alys nudged him with her elbow. "Shut up."

He stopped and looked down the hall both ways before taking her other hand in his. "Before you do go back, I do have one small request." He looked down at the way her hands fit in his. "Don't forget me."

Alys laughed and shook her head. "Oswin—"

"I'm serious, Alys."

"How could I forget any of this, let alone you?"

"Just promise me?"

She nodded, bewildered. "I promise."

Oswin ran his thumbs over her knuckles, trying to satisfy himself with this vow, but he still seemed uneasy. He released one of her hands reluctantly and led her into the Great Hall where Basir and Robin were waiting for them.

"Are we heading to the train station, then?" Alys asked, feeling a wave of nausea sweep over her knowing that her departure had to be so soon. She understood why. She didn't want to put this place in any more danger than she already had, but just because she understood it, just because she *agreed* that she had to leave, didn't mean she liked it.

Robin looked to Basir, who nodded. "I am afraid so." He took Alys's free hand in both of his, the most amiable action he'd ever shown her. "How can we ever thank you for what you have done for us and for Terra Mirum?"

His friendliness towards her took Alys off guard, enough that her other hand left Oswin's so it could awkwardly pat the top of Basir's until he released her. "It's...anyone would have done the same."

"We are forever in your debt," Basir insisted. "And while we cannot do much, we would like to offer you a kind of protection."

"Protection?"

"So that we may defend you as you defended Terra Mirum. From this day onward, as citizens of Elan Vital, we will make it our personal duty to ensure your sleep is never plagued by nightmares again."

Alys blinked and looked to Oswin. "You can do that?"

Oswin smiled a little, but it seemed sad.

"We know it isn't much," Robin started.

"It's more than you know," Alys assured her. "My only regret is I can't stay longer to show my appreciation for all you've done for *me*."

Robin forced a smile, but it too was far too melancholy for anyone to mistake it for genuine. She reached out for Alys, taking her hands in each of her own.

"Robin," Oswin started quietly. "Please..."

"I'm sorry, Your Highness," Robin answered. "It must be done."

"What must be done?" Alys asked.

"If we shadows have offended," Robin started reciting, and Alys could feel something in the air beginning to tense and churn. "Think but this and all is mended."

Alys looked back at Oswin. "What must be done?"

"That you have but slumbered here while these visions did appear."

There was so much Oswin wanted to say, but, instead, he just shook his head helplessly. "I'll see you in your dreams, Alys."

Robin raised two fingers to Alys's forehead. "And this weak and idle theme? No more yielding but a dream."

EPILOGUE

Alys woke to the sound of beeping, and when she opened her eyes the light made her want to shut them again instantly. Her head was pounding, and when she raised a hand to it, she could feel something was lightly pulling on her arm.

"You're awake," a voice breathed in relief, and she heard someone sit up in his chair. "You had me really worried there."

"Brian?" she murmured groggily, trying to open her eyes enough to put a face to the voice.

"Yeah, Alys, it's me."

"Where the hell am I?" Her mouth felt tight, and as she raised her fingers to her lips, she could feel part of her lower lip was swollen and bruised.

"In a hospital just outside of Olympia," Brian answered. "You were in a pretty bad car wreck."

Alys blinked. "What?"

"They said you went off the road and hit a brick wall?"

Alys stared up at the ceiling as uneasiness began to creep in. Her mouth was dry and she licked her lips. It didn't help, only making her tongue taste like iron. "How long have I been out?"

"Only a couple of hours." He set a cool, damp rag on her forehead. "Someone said they saw it happen, called it in immediately. When the ambulance found my number under your emergency contacts on your phone, they called me."

Alys sat up quickly, but the action made her woozy. "I've been here the whole time?"

"Where else would you have been? You were unconscious."

Alys slumped back onto the pillows and closed her eyes.

No.

It wasn't possible.

Her eyes stung with tears and her throat tightened. It couldn't have been just a dream.

She'd been there. She'd stopped the Nightmare and the Jabberwock. She'd spoken with Charlie. She—

Charlie.

"Brian." Alys reached out and took his hand. "There's something you need to know about Charlie."

"I know," he answered, his face falling. "My mom called me this morning about it."

Alys' arm went slack. "Shit." She laughed at her own stupidity. "Your mom. I completely forgot your mom still lives there. Of course, your mom would call you...stupid, Alys..." She closed her eyes and shook her head.

"Is that why you were driving up here? To let me know what happened?"

Alys felt her face flush and she looked down. She'd never felt so foolish. "Not the only reason. It seemed like as good a time as any to leave Appleweed, but..." She shook her head. "Maybe I should have waited until I was fit to drive." Had she really dreamed it? Smoke, Terra Mirum...Oswin? The more she thought on it, the more the details seemed to grow hazy.

Brian misunderstood the melancholy that colored her demeanor. "I'm going to see what it takes to get you out of here today, okay? You can come up and stay in Seattle with me until you figure a few things out. And, in the meantime, we'll talk about Charlie."

She nodded, numb, and he left the room to find a nurse or a doctor. Had she really dreamed it all? The idea caused a wave of nausea to wash over her.

The doctor came and went. Then the nurse came and went. They both prodded and poked at her, took her blood pressure and asked her a series of what seemed like inane questions to check her coherency. Then, after what seemed like hours, the nurse told them she'd been discharged and was free to go.

Alys used one of the bags they'd pulled from the wreckage of her car to dress herself in clean clothing, and when she emerged from the bathroom, Brian was holding a manila envelope.

"What's that?"

"Personal effects that you were wearing

during the time of the crash. Wallet, jewelry, keys..."

"My poor, sad, worthless keys." Alys sighed, reaching for the envelope to tear open the top and turn it upside down on the bed. This resulted in a strange sound, the sound of something metal, something other than her keys dropping onto the bed — something with a chain that trailed behind it. She moved her hands out of the way slowly to look and absolutely froze.

"Alys?" Brian stood from his seat and moved to her, his brow furrowing. He looked from her to the golden pocket watch that lay on the bed with its chain splayed out around it. He looked from the intricate floral etching on the front of the watch to Alys, who didn't dare move. "What is it?"

She slowly reached out and picked up the pocket watch, placing it around her neck and holding it close to her chest. "My flower."

ABOUT THE AUTHOR

It has been said it takes all kinds to make a world. Some people are made of stone, some have hearts of gold, while others consist of sugar and spice.

Kiri was born from ink and stardust.

She enthusiastically prods and catalogues the world around her. She's driven by questions: the whys and what ifs of the world. Her peers call her fickle, seemingly unable to focus on a singular field of study. Every day she's submerged in some new thing, from the unexplained supernatural phenomena to how to make a proper cake pop.

She reads, she cooks, she crafts, and she games. She researches and dabbles in pottery and painting. She hikes through wilderness and wanders through every metropolis she encounters.

She's a writer, a singer, an actor, an adventurer, but, above all, Kiri is curious.

For more information about Kiri, her adventures, other publications, and works, visit:

www.KiriCallaghan.com

Enjoy Other Books By

Doce Blant Publishing
www.DoceBlant.com

Beyond the Last Hill
by David K. Bryant

Hardbound ISBN: 978-0-9978913-3-1
Paperback ISBN: 978-0-9978913-4-8
ePub ISBN: 978-0-9978913-5-5

The Déjà vu Chronicles
by Marti Melville

Midnight Omen (book 1)
Hardbound ISBN: 978-0-9971023-3-8
Paperback ISBN: 978-0-9971023-4-5
ePub ISBN: 978-0-9971023-5-2
Library of Congress Control Number:
2016906558

The Tales of Barnacle Bill: Skeleton Krewe
by Barnacle Bill Bedlam

Hardbound ISBN: 978-0-9967622-3-6
Paperback ISBN: 978-0-9967622-2-9
ePub ISBN: 978-0-9967622-4-3

The Next Victim
by Cutter Slagle

Hardbound ISBN: 978-0-9967622-6-7
Paperback ISBN: 978-0-9967622-5-0
ePub ISBN: 978-0-9967622-7-4

'Til Death
by Cutter Slagle

Hardbound ISBN: 978-0-9978913-0-0
Paperback ISBN: 978-0-9978913-1-7
ePub ISBN: 978-0-9978913-2-4
Library of Congress Control Number:
2016949335

Never Surrender
by Deanna Jewel

Hardbound ISBN: 978-0-9971023-0-7
Paperback ISBN: 978-0-9971023-1-4
ePub ISBN: 978-0-9971023-2-1